CHIPPED BEEF ON TOAST
S. O. S.

By

Charles H. Bertram

Charles H. Bertram 2 Brown Bear Path
Ormond Beach, Florida, USA 32174

CBERTNFL@MSN.COM
www.charleshbertram.com

ISBN 0-7414-1554-2

Published by:

INFINITY
PUBLISHING.COM

1094 New DeHaven Street, Suite 100
West Conshohocken, PA 19428-2713
Info@buybooksontheweb.com
www.buybooksontheweb.com
Toll-free (877) BUY BOOK
Local Phone (610) 941-9999
Fax (610) 941-9959

Printed in the United States of America

Printed on Recycled Paper

Published June 2007

DEDICATION

This book is dedicated to My Wife, Janice,
however, not for her help or encouragement
which was very little, rather because
Janice knows that the way to get me to
do something is to tell me I can't.
And because I love her!

ACKNOWLEDGMENTS

Special thanks to my Air Force buddy
Peter A. Hoetjes for the cover photo,
and the many veterans that gave my story ideas.

CHIPPED BEEF ON TOAST

MY STORY

In high school I was not an academic student. I did graduate in the top half of the lower quarter of the class of 1956. I passed algebra because my track coach in East St. Louis, Illinois, taught it. A skinny small guy like me had better learn how to run. My best subjects were drafting and machine shop. The Air Force recruiter faithfully assured me that the Air Force would send me to drafting school. So I joined for four years rather than let the Army draft me for two years.

At basic training in Texas we had the worst training instructor on Lackland AFB. Since 99 percent of the seventy men in our barracks could read, we all knew that the next day would be spent taking a long series of tests to see how best we were qualified to help our country. It was posted on our bulletin board; yet our T.I. had us up till after three a.m. scrubbing the barracks for some petty reason. Then we were left at the testing area an hour early. We stood in the hot sun till ordered inside of a Quonset hut. Thanks to my working out with the track team the weeks before joining, I was in good shape and stayed awake for the whole six hours of testing. I'm sure many other guys smarter than I did not. After our tests were collected a lieutenant stepped to the front of the room and ordered all the N.C.O.'s and T.I.'s out, with instructions that the last man was to close the door. The lieutenant asked us if there were any suggestions or complaints about the testing. I stood and informed him that we were not tested under the best of conditions, describing the lack of sleep and hot building. I added that this was surely not in the best interest for the Air Force. He thanked me and, when no one else spoke, said we were to stay seated till our T.I. came for us. The first T.I. in the door was mine, who grabbed my shirt and chewed me up and down. That's when I learned why lieutenant is spelled starting with the letters "L I E."

I learned the next day that I had scored too high for drafting school and would be sent to Lowry AFB in Denver for one of the longest RADAR schools in the Air Force. I joined my classmates in taking some college courses at the University of Colorado Extension in Denver. One class was in fiction writing. At Lowry, the RADAR school was a six-hour day. There was no homework since it was all classified.

Our mail room clerk, a Polish kid, had an old car for sale. I told him his price was too low. He said if I could help him find a buyer, he'd split with me what I could get over his first price. I found a buyer, and stood to make a quick $20. Trouble was he let the guy pay him over time and then shipped out before paying what would include my share. I, too, shipped out over a year later, sure I'd never see that twenty.

The Air force was not about to let us have a six-hour day, so we were often subjected to many cruddy details and make-work projects. You could get off those by finding a part-time permanent detail.

The first one I had was as squadron draftsman, but I worked myself out of a job just at the time there was a call for men to be on the Honor Guard. The First Sergeant explained to me that the Honor Guard would carry rifles alongside the flag during parades. To me, that meant I would be one of the first ones to be done. He also threw in that we could be called on to fire rifles at military funerals. It turned out that in a city as large as Denver, there was a funeral on many a Saturday. The only good thing about it was that going to funerals got us out of some inspections.

One Saturday when there was a base-wide inspection, we made our beds and got on a bus with our seven MI Garand rifles and figured not to get back until the inspection was over. That was not to be. It was both short and not far from the base. I should have known something was wrong when our sergeant used his own car instead of riding the bus with us. The bus was heading back to base before ten o'clock. We were in a bind. Our boots were muddy from the cemetery. I came up with an idea; we got off the bus before the base, and boarded a city bus that took us downtown. I marched the men, rifles and all to the nearest VFW club; there I talked the bartender into letting us stay for awhile. We only had bus fare back, and money for a couple pitchers of beer. Then, businessmen who were veterans came in; they began to treat us to beer in exchange for listening to their war stories. It was there that the idea for this book started.

I was in RADAR school so long that when I got to Griffiss AFB in Rome, N.Y., my plane, the F-89, was obsolete. I was frozen in rank, but could get transferred to TDY, temporary duty. I learned that at Alexandria Bay, New York, on the St. Lawrence river, our base special services unit had a fishing camp; you got $180 a month food allowance plus your base pay. At that time my take-home pay was $52 and change, while my car payment was $49.50. I talked them into hiring me, and for the next two years I was in the 1,000 Islands during the summer and on the flight line during the winters.

The first week the camp was open, I learned there was a lot about how things had been done in the past we did not know. The sergeant who had run the camp had died and there were no real records on what should be done. One of my first problems was with the worms. The camp was five miles from town and the nearest bait shop. The boathouse had always sold worms. I was trying to get the base to give me some petty cash, when in the mail I found a surprise; there was a folded new twenty-dollar bill. The mail room guy had traced me down and kept his word. With that twenty I bought worms: 500 worms for five dollars, a bale of moss, and a box of ice cream cardboard containers. I was now in the worm business, but not for profit. I made fifty cents on each sale, and learned that in a little over a week the worms would earn the price of a case of Budweiser, plus a new supply of worms. I shared that beer to great advantage to the Air Force and myself. When I had an outboard motor problem that I could not fix, I did not take it to town and send a bill to the base. My approach was to invite one of the better mechanics to bring his kids, and have a beer with me on his way home or in early evening. Our camp had a fishing dock and a whole set of playground equipment that was seldom used. For a few beers, I would not only get the motor repaired but would learn how to deal with that problem.

The next spring, back at the base, I came close to getting shot because of worms. The snow was melting along the edge of the runway. A guy came into our hanger and said that worms were coming out from under the edge of snow on the sun-warmed concrete. Next thing, a bunch of us that fished were crawling along the runway with old coffee cans, so busy picking up night crawlers that two of us did not see to where we had advanced to. There was a sharp jab at my back. I turned to see an MP with a shotgun, pointing it at my head. He pushed it into my ribs and ordered my buddy and me to follow him. We had gotten too close to the armed "HOT" planes that were in a restricted area. On the way, the MP stumbled and his shotgun went off. It blew a load of dirt on my shoes and caused a load of something else to drop in my shorts. The MP captain was himself, a fisherman, and understood our problem. He let us go and began to chew out the MP that was under orders not to carry his gun with a round in the chamber. That was the closest I ever came to being shot in four years.

THE END

THE PINE TREE

It helps to have served in the military to fully understand my incident with a pine tree. I was in the Air Force attending a long radar school at Lowry Air Force base in Denver, Colorado.

Some classmates and I were rock climbing in the Rocky Mountains near Mt. Evans one-day in early spring. On one of our many stops to catch our breath, I saw a small, perfectly shaped pine tree. It was about three feet high and several hundred feet above the timberline and was growing out of a crack in a rock. I pointed out to my friends that this tree had no business growing there and without soil would soon die, but I was going to save it. I would pull it out and re-plant the tree in good soil below the tree line.

My friends, saying I could not do that ensured the tree's chances for survival. They had lots of reasons, as we sat in the sun at ten thousand feet. I had no tools; the roots would break; it was too big to move; and they added, might be against the law.

That did it! Now I would not only save the tree, but also would take it back to base and plant my tree by our barracks. That announcement set off a great cry, "You can't do that, no Airman Second can just go and plant a tree on the base without permission!"

So I made a wedge of flat rocks and hammered with a big one until the crack opened up and released my tree. Then, with the roots wrapped in moss and snow and carefully held in my field jacket, I left Arapaho National Forest. All the way back to base I carried the tree, as my friends carried on about how much trouble I was getting into.

That night with a bed adaptor, butt can, and fingers, I planted my tree. I put the tree in the only safe spot near Barracks 768. I put it about three feet from the sidewalk in the middle of a small square of grass between our barracks and the orderly room, right near the Major's window. I knew that the tree would be safe there, from formations and football games. For several days the tree got water at night, sun at daytime, and I got assurances that when the Air Force was done with my hide, I would also be paying a big fine to the Park service. In defense I replied that since I had saved the tree, the Park officials would not mind and what could the Air Force do to me, ship me off to the Air Training Command for a long, boring RADAR school?

About four days later when most had forgotten about my tree, there came a message to our classroom. "Airman Bertram will report to the First Sergeant ASAP!" I left for the Office as my classmates patted my back and wished me well in my next base in Greenland or Goosebay. With not just a little apprehension, I headed for the First Sergeant's desk. This would not be my first or even second visit under less than favorable reasons. My

8

timing was definitely not good. Only two weeks before, I had been spokesman for a complaint to the First Sergeant. The Airmen that were on a paint detail with me had failed to convince the sergeant in charge of the painting that we should not paint a certain barracks. I pointed out to him, and later to the First Sergeant that the barracks in question was to be torn down soon, and a parking lot was to be there. The First Sergeant asked me how many stripes I had, and then how many stripes the sergeant in charge of the paint detail had, and if that answered my question. The bulldozer was now at work on that barracks with the paint still wet.

As I walked, I tried to think what I would say; what was a good reason for me to have dug up a tree and plant it near the orderly room. So with sweaty palms and a lump the size of a bowling ball in my throat, I reported.

"Bertram," said the First Sergeant, "did you plant that tree over there?"

"Yes, Sir, I mean yes, Sergeant," I replied. Then he said, "well, the Major thinks you put it too close to the sidewalk, and would it be okay with you if he has it moved over?"

THE END

SCAR.WAF

There are several lessons I learned while in the National Guard of the State of Missouri. One of them, of course, had to do with getting to classes on time and finding out what the whole thing was about. I had just joined the 880th Aviation Engineers of the Missouri National Guard when I went into a class late. We were learning the general orders. Now, General Order #10 stating to salute all officers and colors and standard not cased was no problem. Or, General Order #8 stating to go give the alarm in case of fire or disorder was no problem. But in General Order #7, to talk to no one except in the line of duty; that was a problem.

For three whole days I didn't say a word. Three days of that and I almost flunked out of high school. I had an awful time trying to decide what they meant by "talk to no one except in the line of duty." I had joined the National Guard, and these were the orders of the Guard. When I hadn't said anything in East St. Louis High School for several days, this was something that got the attention of the administration. So, my guidance counselor called me in, and I explained to him that I had taken this oath to follow these orders of the Guard. Fortunately, he had been in the service himself and he explained to me that these were the orders of guard duty, not just the Guard. He could have waited until I got out of the office before he started laughing and calling the other teachers over. But nevertheless, I got past that.

Now, the 880th Aviation Engineers were a SCARWAF Outfit, and I was confused at first, because we had army rank, army uniforms, army officers, except the one Air Force liaison officer who wore his blue uniform. Then we had blue Air Force construction equipment, and our paychecks were blue Department of the Air Force paychecks.

It seemed as though when they created the United States Air Force out of the old Army Air Corps, there were engineer battalions in reserve that were hard to decide which group would get them. So they created a temporary Special Category Army Reserves with Air Force, and that was the outfit I was in.

There were several puzzling things about that outfit, and I learned several lessons our first summer at summer camp in Wisconsin. We had the Army saying we were going to go to Fort Leonard Wood, Missouri, and the Air Force saying we were going to Wisconsin. The Army said we outrank the Air Force, but the Air Force said "you send them to Leonard Wood and we won't pay them and they'll know that before they go." So we went to Wisconsin.

One of the things I was puzzled about all the time in the service was if there was one truth, it was that the men would gripe about doing something stupid. They do things stupidly, of course, but they would gripe. Yet, when we went to camp, we loaded up several trucks with oil drums; big round, 55-gallon drums marked "aviation fuel." Now, we were an aviation engineer battalion. We were supposed to build runways and roads adjacent to them for airports. But why we were carrying aviation fuel from St. Louis to Wisconsin was beyond me. The fact that we loaded these drums on the trucks with nobody complaining was puzzling.

But I did learn a lesson on that, and I also learned why they do not give guys on guard duty live ammo that same night. I was Corporal of the Guard, and with the Sergeant of the Guard in a jeep; we were going out into the back wooded area where we had our ammo dump. All of our oil drums had been unloaded and stored; trucks sat around; and there was all of our explosive equipment. We got there and found no guard on duty.

The sergeant said, "oh, he's asleep in one of these trucks. Boy, is he in trouble!"

Then, suddenly out of the woods this terrified, young, 17-year-old boy came running, just scared to death. You could tell by the look on his face that he was upset.

The first thing he said was, "do you guys have any live ammo? You got any bullets?"

Sergeant said, "What do you want with bullets?"

I said, "You don't need any bullets."

He says, "No, no, I'm under attack."

I laughed and said "Who's attacking you, the owls?"

He says, "No, no, there are people out in the woods throwing rocks at me and I don't have any bullets."

We said, "there's nobody throwing rocks at you. It's 11:30 at night and in the middle of the woods in Wisconsin miles from anywhere."

He said, "No, no, no," and he was really scared.

So we started looking around and then, "BANG!" I heard a pop and then "BANG!" another one.

The duty guard said, "there, there, over there. They're doing it from that side, now."

The sergeant looked at me, and I looked at him. I knew by the look on his face that he knew what I knew; that what the boy thought was people throwing rocks at him was just the oil drums cooling off and popping from the temperature change.

The sergeant, having trouble keeping a straight face, turned to me and said "Are you going to tell him, or should I tell him?"

I said "Oh, I'll tell him." I put my hand on the boy's shoulder and said "Now, young man, (and I was only a year older than he was) you don't need any bullets. For one thing that truck right over there is just filled with hand grenades."

Well, the sergeant didn't like my sense of humor and before I could get any further and explain about the oil drums, I got whacked over the head with a nightstick. Then I was told to take the young boy's place while the sergeant took him back to calm him down and put him on another guard post.

As soon as the sergeant left, I was sitting there nursing my head. I walked over to those stupid oil drums that were sitting there that we had brought all the way from St. Louis. I kicked one of them and it made a thud. I kicked another one and it made a rattling sound.

Now, I always had learned that engineers always took care of their own and always could be considered a good group to be around, compared to other outfits, but that rattling sound puzzled me. Then I saw that some of the oil drums had spigots, but others had a clamp-type lid where the whole lid would come off. One of those was the one that rattled. Well, it didn't take long to find some tools, and take a lid off and shine my flashlight down to discover as 55-gallon can filled with 12-ounce cans of St. Louis-made Anheuser-Busch Budweiser beer that had come with our unit.

Now I knew why nobody complained about that, and I learned why they don't give bullets to young kids on guard duty.

THE END

A MOP FOR THE GENERAL

"Uncle Charlie, what did you do in the war? Before I could say there was no war when I was in the Air Force, my wife called out. "He fixed boat motors for the Air Force!"

"Well, did you do anything brave?" my nephew asked. I started to tell him about the time that I planted a tree on the base, when I remembered the time that I got a General to do my mopping. Most GI's would love to hand their mop just to a sergeant. Yes, I handed a mop to a general and he did my mopping.

It all started because the needs of the Air force for people to repair certain planes did not line up with the men that were coming out of training schools and those that were getting their discharge. I was one that got transferred back and forth from one RADAR school to another. By the time I completed a school, my plane was obsolete.

When I reached the flight line at Griffiss Air Force Base in upstate New York, I was surplus, frozen in rank, but eligible to be loaned out TDY, Temporary Duty.

I managed to get loaned to Special Services, the recreation department of the Air Force. In those days, Special Services operated a recreation fishing camp at Alexandria Bay, New York. It was funded by the use of non-appropriated funds, the profit from base movies and service clubs. At the camp, serviceman and their families could use cabins and a fleet of boats and outboard motors. Alexandria Bay is in the center of the 1,000 Islands on the banks of the St. Lawrence River. Our camp was near town, but on an inlet with great fishing.

The camp also had six house trailers fixed up as cabins for the top officers and other VIP's. I developed a VIP policy that seemed to work. They could have anything or service that we could supply, but they had to ask for it. We tried to let them have as much privacy as possible. This also gave me more time for my work.

One day a certain general informed me he wanted a boat and motor for the next day. In the past he never came early, so I was not in any great rush to get his ready. I asked my helper who was changing spark plugs, not to rent out one of the newer motors. It rained the night before, so I was up at five, pumping and mopping water out of forty boats. I had held back on a boat with a new motor for the General, and was planning to mop it and check the motor when I got done with the early crowd. A party who could not get his motor started interrupted me. I was sitting on the back of a boat with a fuel pump in my hands when the General showed up. He asked if I had his boat ready. I was trying to explain to him that it still needed to be mopped and was putting down the fuel pump with one hand and grabbing a mop with the other. Then the general said "You are busy, let me have the mop." So I handed it to him and went back to my job. All was going well until his aide, a Second Lieutenant, came by. He saw what was happening and yelled at me: "The General is over there using a MOP! And here you are, playing with some motor parts. What the hell is going on?" I just could not pass up the chance, so I said "Don't worry, Sir, the General will do a good job!" I thought it was funny. The Lieutenant did not; in fact, I was worried he would have a heart attack. Aware of the conflict, the General quietly rowed his boat away from the dock.

Most likely, I would have gotten away with my remark and getting the General to use my mop, except in the confusion, I let the General take his boat into the St. Lawrence River with a motor that had no spark plugs.

THE END

HOSPITAL WARD 5

My adventures in base hospital Ward 5 started when I learned that our December 31st paycheck was going to be held up till two days after New Year's Eve. The new base commander decided that it would be better for so many young men away from home on their first New Year's if they had less money. Less money? My pay was $52; and my car payments were $49. Thanks to a connection in payroll, I learned early that the no-pay rumor was true. I beat it to the first blood bank to sell a pint of blood for the $10 going rate. That was on a Saturday morning. By noon the rate was down to $5.

At the nearby Army Hospital, I rolled up my right sleeve. It had only been a week since I gave blood to get a day off. I usually gave from my left arm, but didn't want the army nurse to see the needle mark. After you pumped out your pint, they gave you a payout slip and a one-hour wait before it was good. I was reading a magazine and drinking juice when a good-looking young WAF (Women Air Force) joined me.

We were talking about New Year's Eve plans, when she went to put her juice cup back on the table. I saw her knees (I looked a lot at legs) were folding in! She was starting to faint. I jumped up and like a hero, caught her. I got a good grip tactfully around her waist. The last thing I could recall was her breast sliding through my hands as we both hit the floor and knocked over the drink table. The effort was too much for me. I, too, had fainted. We both ended up on those rolling cots they use. A lot of staff seemed to be making fun of us. The merriment ended when the head Doctor came in, looked us over and stated, "don't pay them for four hours." Then to be sure, he took our pay slips and changed the time on them. The WAF was mad at me! As if it was my fault!

A few days later, what I thought was a long hangover turned out to be much more. I was sick as a dog. It was my turn for six-to-twelve guard duty at the orderly room front door. I never made it. Sometime after eleven, I passed out. They took me to the base hospital in a jeep. One minute I was dressed, on guard duty, and the next thing I knew, was when I woke up dressed in an open-back blue cotton garment, in a bed, in a world of white, and behind bars! A nurse saw that I was awake, and quickly told me that the door was not locked. I had measles and had to be isolated, and the only isolation bed that was available was the one for stockade customers. With a weak voice, I informed her that I'd had measles. "Well, you have a high fever and a rash and will stay in isolation till the doctor sees you," she replied.

Later that day, it was decided that I had mononucleosis, "the kissing disease," as it was called. The only treatment I got was two aspirins and as much water as I wanted, and two or more weeks of bed rest. Two girls then came into my room. One was a nurse's aide and the other one was some kind of volunteer, like a candy striper. They carried a wash pan and stuff, and put up a privacy screen. "You are getting a sponge bath!" The older of the two informed me. She asked me to roll to one side and she spread a rubber sheet and put it under me. I must have closed my eyes, as I worried about what came next. Then, just as suddenly as they appeared, a large black man, a male aide who told me to take off my robe replaced them. He saw the look in my eyes. "What did you think those girls were going to do to you?" I didn't answer. He handed me a wet washcloth and said, "I don't do privates." When I did nothing, he pointed to my crotch and made a washing motion. I complied and said that "if you don't do privates, do you do sergeants?"

He had me roll over, but stopped from washing my back when he saw the rash. He called to the nurse. "Are you sure this kid is not contagious?" He asked.

"Only if you kiss him," was the reply.

I was moved to ward Number 5, the convalescing ward, for two weeks of bed rest and observation. That ward had a large number of guys with rheumatic fever due, in part, to the high altitude of Denver, and for many, the fact that they missed getting penicillin shots for strep throat.

In Ward 5, we had an easy life, plus we got to see, be near, dream about, and talk to Lt. Nurse Dixie. She must have wondered how come so many of us were from the south. Her coming our way was accompanied by hums of the song "Dixie." What the boys were singing was the first line over and over (I Wish I Was in Dixie...."). She had the face of an angel and was built like a brick tool shed.

Also on the staff was a doctor who was a blood specialist with a last name that sounded somewhat like "Screw-loose." Because of my "mono," he and his aide who we called "The Leech" took many samples of my blood. I asked if he had an anemic friend in another ward I was supporting. "No, I put it on my rose garden; you should see how red they are." I made plans to visit his off-base house someday, but never did.

But the days were long, and we had only a few old magazines that the Red Cross old ladies would bring once in awhile. They also gave out cigarettes, and guys could go out to a glassed-in porch and smoke, even the ones with rheumatic fever. I gave my joints away or traded for a bottle of Coke. They were old four-packs, old Luckies and Camels. The Luckies came in green and red boxes. The green was the older, and was too dry to smoke unless steamed.

There was a Coke machine (five cents a small bottle), in the front lobby. We could not take the glass bottles back to our ward, but could take out our individual water pitchers to fill with Coke out there. These were ceramic, white, one-quart size with a lid. One boring day I called a buddy and had him hide a pint of rum in the lobby phone booth. Soon my buddies in one end of Ward 5 were having Rum and Coke for our private happy hour each afternoon. The little plastic pill cups just held a full shot. I figured the rum would do no more harm than the smoking.

For training purposes, the base hospital took part in a simulated plane crash exercise. Guys would be placed out on the runway with red tags on them. The tags listed their condition, such as 50% body burns, broken leg, bleeding, and so on. The hospital had to go and bring them back, and mark on the tag what treatment and the time. Our ward was not considered to be contagious, so the overflow of guys on stretchers soon filled the space between our beds. We were; on the whole, glad for something to break the monotony. Lt. Nurse Dixie had to climb over some of the smiling guys as she moved to the back end of the ward. One look at her and guys were asking us how to get placed here for a few weeks.

Several hours later when the exercise was over, there was a meeting just outside our ward, as the actions of the hospital staff was evaluated. I could only hear part of what was going on, and was not interested till I heard Lt. Nurse Dixie raise her voice in protest. Then, there was a great roar of laughing. And a very red-faced Doctor Screw-loose rushed by on his way to the parking lot.

What had caused the uproar was, Dr. Screw-loose put his foot in his mouth big time. He had given a low grade to Nurse Dixie to the effect he did not observe her being very active. She protested that she was, and that he could not see her, and made no effort to get to the back end of the ward. Another doctor, trying to be helpful, asked Screw-loose if maybe he had observed her without her knowing it. "No!" He said. "When I observe a nurse at her work, I always expose myself. I mean, I let them see me!" But his correction was too late. And word about his statement spread throughout the hospital faster than any strep germ.

When they said I was ready to return to duty, the staff of Ward 5 wished me well, and remarked how good my stories were for the morale. You see they never learned about the Rum and Coke.

THE END

BIKE TALES

"Hurry up and wait, that's all we do," said the tired PFC as he kicked mud off the edge of his boots and picked up his pack and MI.

"Come on, you guys; quit the bitching," said the Sergeant. "We've been told by the lieutenant to wait down by the road. A truck will come by just to save your poor little pink feet; you bunch of sissies!" The corporal was always busting them, yet most had been in combat for months fighting their way north up the boot of Italy. Their fighter team was down to six since they pulled back, following two weeks on the line.

"Anybody got a butt? I'm dying for a smoke," said Private Mack Williams as he leaned his bar against a tree and sat on his pack.

"Just where would any of us buy a cigarette?" Replied PFC Grant, as he joined the rest all sitting by the side of the road. They sat there and looked at each other, tired of each other's stories, and Private Grant reached into his pack, unrolled a bunch of paper and pulled out a fresh new pack of Lucky Strikes.

"Where did you get those?" yelled Private Smith.

"Off a German. Off a dead Kraut. They're not

beat up too bad."

"What'll we do, divide 'em up?"

"I have a better idea," said PFC Kowalski. "Let's have a contest. We'll tell stories. The guy with the best story gets the whole pack. He can share if he wants to." Several nodded in agreement.

"Stories about what?"

"I don't know. How long we gotta wait here?" Griped Private Grant.

"Well," said Private Brown, "if I had a bike, I could run up the road and find out, but I don't have a bike. I had a bike once."

"We all had bikes," said Grant.

"Hey!" Said Smith; "anybody got a story about a bicycle? Let me see the hands of all the guys who have a story about a bicycle." Four hands went up. "All right, there's our contest."

"Well, wait a second. What about Private Johnson?"

"All right, he can be the judge. It's a deal. While we're waiting for the truck, we'll all tell our best stories about bicycles, and the one with the very best story gets the pack of cigarettes."

First was Private Brown. "Well, you see, I had a bicycle; it wasn't very good. And I was up north of St. Louis on top of a hill called 'Signal Hill.' I started coming down the hill, and that was also Highway 50, and the chain came off my bike right in the middle of traffic. First thing you know I'm dragging my feet, trying to slow down, but that's not working. With no chain, I don't have any brakes, you know. But when I hit 89th Street, I was going about 40 miles an hour; went right through the red light dodging cars, and I realized I've got a long straight hill and road all the way down to the inner city, and I'm flying. And I'm starting to get scared. Then about 50 miles an hour or so, I guess, (it was a 45 mile-an-hour speed limit section there,) I was passing cars left and right. There were too many parked cars 'cause something was going on at a church there and I couldn't get off the highway, then I was going too fast to try and make a sharp turn. I dragged my feet till my sneakers got hot. Then I passed this police car and I got a little bit farther down and I saw a train way ahead. So in desperation, I bumped over the sidewalk; went into a grassy lawn; and then jumped off the back of the bike, falling on my rear end. The bike crashed into a fence. Let me tell you, the police stopped. They came up to me, and I thought I was in trouble. They said, 'You okay?' and I said, 'I'm fine.' They said they'd put the bike in their trunk and take me back home. They said I was going 60 miles an hour. None of you guys went 60 miles an hour on a bicycle! That's my story."

"Well," said Private Smith, "I had a bike when I was going to junior college, a good bike, and somebody stole it. So I bought another bike, not quite as good. I put a big hard chain around a tree and I came back just in time to see some kids with a hacksaw just about done cutting through my chain. So I said, "this is not good." So I took the bike home, and in the garage, my Dad had these little cans of paint. So I got some tape and, you know those yellow and black barricades the police use? I painted that whole bike broad yellow and black diagonal stripes top to bottom. Never locked it up after that. Nobody ever stole it. I just rode it and leaned it against a tree. If somebody borrowed it, I'd hear about it. They'd say, 'Hey,' I saw a guy on your bike. Did you let him use it?' Well, that was my bike story."

Johnson thought a minute and said "I've got one! When I was about, let's see 13 or so, my older brother, he's two years older than me and a bunch of his buddies came over on bicycles and they went somewhere, I don't know, shooting, I think, with a 22. Anyway, Mother asked me to go and get her some stuff from the grocery story. My bike wasn't working. So, without the other guy's permission, I took one of their bikes and started for the store. Just as I'm turning into the street to go to the store, this car came out of a parking space and rammed right into me. I never saw him coming. He clobbered me head-on. He knocked me down, skinned my elbows, but he ran over the bike and it was not my bike. I was upset, you know, probably tearing a little bit. And the man was all upset about hitting me, because he knew it was his fault. He wanted to take me to the hospital. I said, 'No, I can go home. I just need some band-aids.' What about this bike— it's not even mine, I'm in deep trouble. So what did he do? He threw the bike in the trunk, drove me to Western Auto Store and bought a brand new Schwinn bike and took me home. So then, when my brother's buddies came back, one kid said, 'Where's my bike?' I pointed to the new Schwinn and said, 'Here it is; this is your bike, and I told him about my accident. After that at school, guys were always coming up to me and saying, 'Hey, Johnson, any time you want to borrow a bike, you can have mine.' Okay, that's my tale. Kowalski, what have you got to say?"

"You see, I guess it was on a bicycle at around age 12, I had my first 'hard-on.' They all started laughing. "You guys know, if you give somebody a ride on a bike, if you've got a bar on a man's bike, you can sit them on that like sidesaddle on a horse, but you can't do that with a girl's bike, can you? You see, one day we had this 15-year-old girl, a tomboy; I mean tough as could be, but 'built.' She lived across the street from me. Well, she came riding up to me on her bike, a girl's bike, and said they needed me for a baseball game down the block. Now, 'down the block' meant a ways down the block, and for me to get on my bike and follow her. The game was starting and they needed me for second base. I said my bike was not working. She said, 'Well, I'll give you a ride.' Well, on a girl's bike, if you're gonna give somebody a ride, you have to have them sit on the handlebars while the driver steers, but she had a basket on her handlebars.

So I asked her how she was going to do that. She said, 'I'll show you.' And she leaned the bike over and said, 'You sit on the seat and hold on behind the seat with your hands, and I'll pump the bike standing up.' So that's the way we took off, except that she's pumping the bike and we're riding. Her toush is bouncing into my crotch every time she'd bend down a little. She saw that, and I began to get all excited. I had these thin, old, cheap jeans on and there was no mistaking what was happening. So pretty soon, she started getting embarrassed and she'd try hard and stand up. Any time she had to hit on her brakes, she was back on top of me. Well, by the time we got to the ballgame, I was a wreck! She was mad! And then that night I had my first 'wet dream.' All right, who can top that?"

Grant reached over and tossed Kowalski the cigarettes and said, "You win, hands down." But Grant really got excited about that.

When they finally got a leave, a 48-hour pass to go into Rome, while the other guys were busy entertaining themselves, he was looking all over for a girl's bicycle. He had seen an Army nurse with a cute toush and had envisioned this plan of taking her for a bike ride and hurting his ankle and having her riding back. He never found the bike or the nurse.

THE END

BARRACKS NO. 805

The American serviceman has many outstanding qualities that include a mischievous sense of humor, an irreverent attitude towards authority, natural ingenuity, and creative ways of thwarting rules and regulations. It was Kipling who said, "Single men in barracks are not plaster saints." The learning of technical skills gives rise to unique use of these qualities, such as in Barracks 805 of the 49th Student Squadron. A group of about seventy young airmen enrolled in a long, boring RADAR school where the class day was six hours, and there were three shifts to each weekday.

Barracks 805 was one of eight of the 49th. Each barracks had attached to the end lower bay wall a six inch-square intercom speaker/receiver known affectionately as the "squawk or bitch" box. This communication device made it possible for the orderly room to reach out and inform the men when they needed something done. Inane announcements were also common. The word 'detail' was applied to any (usually meaning- less) bit of work, and the men hated it when a call came on the bitch box, asking who was there and requesting a few good men. Sometimes it was of great importance, like removing weeds near the far runway lights. Other times, it might mean picking up butts near the Officer's Club.

One day Wilson, a bright young airman from

Chicago was working on a Heath-kit electronic model when a voice came over the hated bitch box, saying that the movie had been changed. "One of these days I'm going to have to fix that thing," he said as he pointed his soldering iron towards the bitch box.

"But it works fine," replied Meyers, the assistant barracks chief.

"That's the problem," said Wilson.

"Won't do you any good," said a guy shining his boots. "In a few days they would put in a new one, if you break it."

"The trick is not to break it, just turn it down," said Wilson, as he moved a footlocker and chair. With his improvised ladder, he undid the wires and the one support screw. He studied the circuit board for only a few seconds, and then set it aside to dig in the shoebox of old electrical parts left over from numerous projects. He read off the color code of two resistors, one, a part of the bitch box, and a larger one from his supply. "Let's see, B B R O Y G B V G W," he recited the one-to-ten number color code, using the easy-to-remember poem, *Bad Boys Rape Our Young Girls But Violet gives willingly.* Bad = 1; boys =2; and so on. Once he determined the size he needed, he drilled two holes and installed two new pins and added a resistor parallel to the speaker/mike phone.

Once the modified box was installed, a test had to be made. One of the guys who encouraged

Wilson went to the orderly room and asked the question, "What was the previous announcement? The intercom's box was not very clear. Maybe the volume was set too low." The test and many others all resulted in the same problem. If they called Barracks 805, all they got was "what was that? I can't hear you!" Then, in frustration, the call would go to some other barracks where the communication was better. Once a civilian expert was sent to check it out. He could not find anything wrong, and thought the entire system was too old and would be happy to bid on replacing it.

Another opportunity to test their new electronic training was when an off-base firm got the contract to install pay-television sets in any barracks that wanted one. The TV was coin-operated, with a metal box on one side. Put in a quarter and the set would run for an hour. In less than two days, the set had a note over the coin slot: "Don't put in any money, just plug in or unplug to operate." After awhile the note was removed. At the end of one month, a man came to take out the coins. He got all of seventy-five cents, yet the time meter read over two hundred hours. His complaint to the first sergeant fell on deaf ears, so the set was taken away. It was replaced by one that Wilson got free from someone who had a set that was not worth fixing, according to the TV store.

The highlight of the crew of Barracks 805 had to be the new Coke machine. The old bottle machine on the back porch of the orderly room was replaced with a new liquid, many-flavor, paper-cup machine. Soon a rumor went around that if you knew how, it would dispense Rum and Coke. After a time the first sergeant heard, and tried it. All he could get was plain Coke, and he noted that the root beer mix was always out of order. As always happens, some brown-nose told him to look for a small note on the back of the Coke machine. The note read: *For Rum and Coke, put in two quarters, dropping them both before the first one clicks. Then hold down both the Coke and the root beer button; hold the root beer button for only a second. Note: longer will not give you more rum, but might mess up our controls.* DON'T TELL ANYONE!

The Coke Company representative didn't believe the sergeant till he got a cup of Rum and Coke. He stood and looked at the insides of the machine for so long that the sergeant spoke. "What's the matter, can't you see what my boys did?"

It's not that, I can see what it does and why it works, just, I can't figure how they did it. Our best men tried for years to make a machine put out mixed drinks at our Christmas parties. They never could get one to work right. Any chance I could talk to the guys who set this up?

The sergeant just shook his head. "No, I don't think so. I suggest you go back to a glass bottle machine.

THE END

THE LONGEST DAY
(In 1954)

I asked if I could buy him a beer. "Sure, Kid" he said. He was of the strong-works outdoors type. A tattoo of a nude lady, covered in part by belts of machine gun shells was on his forearm. His face was sun-darkened except for white at the top of his forehead where the shade of a baseball cap blocked it out.

I asked the Veteran what he thought of the film on the Normandy landings, THE LONGEST DAY. His reply was something like this:

"The longest day? I'll tell you about the longest day. For me it was not in 1944, but after the Korean War, about 1953. I had my butt kicked from one end of Korea to the other. Oh, we did little kicking ourselves, but anyway, I still had to do a couple years reserve time. You'd think that after three years of combat I'd have served enough.

"I joined this National Guard outfit that met at Jefferson Barracks in St. Louis. It was the 880th Engineer Battalion and unlike most weekend warriors, they met every Monday night. That suited me, as I got in many hours overtime on weekends. I was a carpenter then. If you did miss a meeting, you could make it up by coming in on Saturday. That is what I did on what was my longest day.

"Because we were an Engineer unit, we did a lot of the repair and maintenance for the base. I came in one Saturday and was asked to fix some leaks in the roof on one of those old wood barracks. You know the kind: the Army has built them the same for years, no matter what the climate, two story with a 5-pitch roof. It was a roof that would take far more snow load than they would ever see in St. Louis. They gave me this eighteen-year old kid as a helper. I said I would rather work alone, but gave in when I saw the heavy old 32-foot wooden ladder. All the shingles, tools and tar were in a 3/4-ton truck. We put the ladder up from one side about eight that morning. By ten-thirty it was getting hot as hell on that roof and I was within a-half hour of being done, so I would not let the Kid take a break. If we did, then it would be even hotter when we got back, I told him. Besides, a little wind had come up. That wind got strong in a hurry. I heard a crash and the Kid yelled "our ladder just fell over."

"It was resting on some tall bushes about ten feet below us. All I could do was to tell the Kid to wave and yell for help at the passing cars, while I finished tarring around the chimney.

"No one was stopping, some just waved back and went on their way. As it got closer to noon, I was sure we could get help as the secretaries went to lunch. None did; it was Saturday, I remembered. I yelled my head off when I saw our top Sergeant go by on his way home. No one came and when it got to be after two, I was getting sunburned and desperate. The Kid said he had an idea.

'If we tie our belts and nail aprons with both our shirts and my claw hammer, maybe I can hook the ladder and pull it within reach.'

"I did the tying so the knots would hold, but we were still about four feet short; so next, both our pants were added to the line. It looked good. The Kid was laying flat just over the edge, with me holding him. I made him wrap the belt around his hand and told him not to let go. He got the ladder part way up and it fell back because the hammer was not hooked too well. When it fell back the ladder fell a few inches into the bush and before I could warn him, the Kid was holding the tip of the belt; With sweaty hands, he lost the whole line when he pulled too hard and it slipped from his grasp. Now we were on the roof in just our shorts, him with jockey and me with my boxer type. Another hour of sunburn and I was thinking that maybe my wife would come looking before dark.

"I saw some MP's in a jeep. I hid behind the chimney and threw the Kid my boxer shorts to wave. He jumped up and down, waving them like a great white flag, and it worked. They saw us. When the jeep got closer, I told the kid to throw me my shorts. He did, but the wind caught them and they blew off the roof. Now I'm hiding between the chimney and the top of the roof bare-ass naked.

"The stupid MP's called the fire department instead of picking up the ladder. The fire truck with its horn and flashing lights got people from all over. I'm trying to hide my bare ass behind the chimney but now, people are starting to be on all sides. I told the Kid he could give me his tee shirt or I would throw him off the roof. With my shoestrings I made the tee shirt into kind of diaper to cover my ass. And down the fire truck ladder we went to cat calls and cheers from the crowd. Thank God there was no one with a camera.

"At the enlisted men's bar, for months I was offered free drinks if I'd wear my diaper. Now that was a long day."

THE END

CIVIL WAR SHOTGUN

A double-barreled shotgun hangs above the fireplace at the summer cottage in the mountains of Tennessee. It's a 10-gauge muzzleloader that uses percussion caps. One rainy day I got my grandfather to tell me about that gun.

"You see," he said, "that gun is the reason we have this land." He was talking about the 160 acres of ridge land that was used for hunting, fishing, and family vacations. There were a few summer cottages on parts that the family had sold off over the years, but for the most part it was known as the Warren land.

"How did that shotgun get the land? Did he fight the Indians with it?" I asked.

"My father, your great-grandfather, was in the war. You call it the Civil War. To him it was always 'The War' although the Indians were long gone when he bought this land from a war-made widow. He raised eight children in the house that burned down a few years back. The shotgun was what did it. He was my daddy. You never met him. Just as well, he was a mean old cuss. Most of us boys left home as soon as we could. What are you pointing to the gun for? I'll get to it. The rain will be with us all day. You're John, right? Okay, John, I'll tell you about that gun.

"Great grandfather was a sniper. He had a heavy barreled gun that could hit a man over 600 yards. You see most men did not like snipers. It was not considered a proper way to fight, but his general, a real Southern gentleman, felt differently. He had been trained at West Point. Lots of sergeants and young officers would be leading them when a fight happened. The sniper's job was to get rid of them. So like I said, men on both sides respected, feared and hated snipers. Your great-grandfather didn't have a lot of friends anyway. As the fight got down to close range, they would be looking for the man with a big heavy gun that had a scope on it. So my daddy also carried that double-barreled 10-gauge shotgun. He loaded a full charge of buckshot and had two shots at a time when all but a few guns were single shot."

"He must have been very strong to march with both the heavy sniper rifle and the shotgun," said the boy. "He told me he got to have a horse, said Grandpa."

"His story of getting rich enough to buy land started just three days before the war was over. He and what was left of the rebel army were running from Grant in Virginia. He was part of a rear guard. Just before dark they got a few miles ahead of the bluecoats. He went to the stream for water. As soon as he had leaned both his guns on a big oak tree and was filling his canteen, he heard horses. He ducked behind the tree and two men rode up. They were the lowdown dirty scavengers, the Union deserters.

They were no part of the army, just mean men that killed and stole from houses where all the men were gone to war. The leader sat on a fine horse and had a new Spencer-repeating rifle. The other had a Colt pistol. Great-grandfather says he cocked both the shotgun and the rifle, but left the shotgun behind the oak tree. Then when they got down from their horses, Grandpa shot the one with the Spencer rifle and then acted like he was reloading. He had the ramrod out and his trick worked. The one with the pistol began to run at him to get within pistol range before he could reload. Your great-grandfather says the man got a sick look on his face when he saw the shotgun aimed at him, as he was halfway across the creek; then he had no face. And Grandpa almost had no shoulder. Both barrels of that 10-gauge had gone off at the same time. That was the only killing I ever heard him talk about. After reloading, Grandpa says he went through their stuff, and their leader had a lot of gold and some pearls and rings, lots of rings, and some federal paper money. Rings that must have been taken from dead men. Well, your Grandpa liked to say 'I was no fool to think I could ever get that stuff back to the rightful owners, so I hid it in my pack and led the horses back to our camp. The better horse had an old brand and an army brand on top of it. There were two hams and some black-eyed beans and a loaf of real bread and some jars of canned peaches in one of the saddlebags. There were also two bottles of whiskey. Back at camp, he sent one horse, a ham and some peaches to General Lee. A young officer came back with thanks and asked where they came from. So Grandpa told them, but said nothing about the money and jewels. He thought for awhile about it, where he could hide the stuff. He came up with the idea of hiding the stuff in the two barrels of the shotgun. Most of the gold coins he heated and bent with his bullet mold so they fit in the shotgun. The bigger coins and pieces of gold he melted into balls and said he rolled the paper money and put it down the barrel last. He did this in his tent while the men ate and drank the whiskey."

The lieutenant rode up and asked if there was any ham left. "We move out soon and it's a race to the next railroad line. There will be supplies for us there. Our troops have no food and little ammunition. The Yanks get there first, and then it will be that the war is over," he said as he rode off.

"Grandpa said that he looked at the sad condition of the rebel army and figures no way could we run a race with the Yankees. Their horses were fed oats. Ours were lucky to get a few bites of grass. He picked up the shotgun. He discovered it was too heavy and if anyone picked it up they would know something was amiss. So it was not a good hiding place after all, and if the Yanks won, he would likely have to give up all guns anyway. Before they moved out, he made the other men stay out of the tent, and he wrapped the shotgun with a rubber sleeping cloth and buried it. He cut the sod with a knife and put the dirt on his shirt; when he was done, not even an Indian could see where the shotgun was hidden. He watered the grass that he had cut. When they took the tent down, he rode off with the rest looking back for trees and rocks so he'd know just where the place was.

"Later that same day there was yelling and cries of anger as word spread that General Lee had given up. Grandpa stayed back and waited to see how it would work. He learned that some men got to keep a horse if they could claim it was their own. And the officers could get to keep their side arms. He still had the pistol from the second scavenger. You see he looked for the lieutenant officer who he had given the horse and ham to, and talked him into promoting Grandpa into an officer. In fact, the lieutenant made him a captain since he had a set of captain's bars he was holding onto for himself. Grandpa had to leave the sniper rifle by the side of the road and was able to tell a Yank that this was his horse taken by the Yankees and re-branded. They let him keep it. Grandpa rode home to find all his relatives had moved out and there was no work, nothing but Yankee soldiers taking all they could get. He found a tailor and had him make him a black suit and a white collar. Then as a preacher, he dug up the shotgun and with it in one hand and a Bible in the other, drove right past all the Yankee patrols till he got to Baltimore. There were only a few times he was asked about a preacher with a gun, and he told them that 'I have to eat just like you. I only shoot the birds and rabbits 'cause all I have is fine shot.' They believed him—a preacher wouldn't lie.

"At Baltimore, he found a distant cousin and left the shotgun with them and he traded the horse for a ticket up to New York. There he went to work for the railroad and waited for two years. Then he wrote letters and found that since Tennessee was a border state, the federal control wasn't as bad as it was in the southern states, so he could go back. He told folks he'd been to the gold field out west and that's where he got his money. He bought this farm from some widow. She was glad to sell it and thanked him and told him about her younger sister who had also lost her man in war. He married that sister and hung the shotgun right there after he built this cabin in 1868. I think he might have used it to hunt with till shot shells were invented."

THE END

CORPORAL HIGGINS

Corporal Brian Higgens put a cover on his Remington, as in "typewriter," not "rifle," and headed for the chow hall, waving and smiling at the other clerks. He had every reason to be happy. Not many soldiers in 1943 had duty like Higgens. His was a dream assignment. A clerk typist, assistant Company clerk stationed at the very safe Granite City Army Supply Depot less than forty miles from his home, and was Corporal in only nine months. He had his own private room at the end of the almost empty barracks since many of the supply staff had families and lived off base.

When drafted, Brian Higgens gave serious consideration to many methods that would keep him out of the Army or combat. There was the option of having one eardrum pierced for a fee, available in South St. Louis; a train trip to the woods of Canada, or moving to a town where the draft board would take a bribe to make you 4-F. Higgens had a good reason to consider those options. His deep fear, that so few knew about, that had been a part of his life for as long as he could remember, made the idea of infantry duty an impossibility. Incredibly, a recruiter that stopped at the high school had given him the idea. A crash course in typing and office management from a nearby trade school, was his salvation.

Lieutenant Churchill stopped Higgens at the chow hall door. The Lieutenant's only connection to the great leader of England was the spelling of his last name. All of the offices knew that, but somewhere in the chain of command, it was decided to play it safe, and so the good Lieutenant was posted here at the Granite City depot. It was a storage and supply depot located on the Illinois side of the Mississippi River just upstream and across from St. Louis, with all it's shopping, ballparks, and many big city advantages.

"Corporal, can I ask you to do me a favor this afternoon?" Now, what do you think his clerk is going to say?

"Glad to, Sir. What do you need, Sir" was the reply from Higgens.

"My wife has to go to the dentist in Alton, and I can't get away. She is afraid to drive back alone because of the drugs. Could you use my car and take her? All you have to do is drive the company jeep to my apartment and use my Buick for the trip. Her appointment is at 14:00 hours, you know, two o'clock, so you should be at my place by one twenty at the latest. It's a half-hour drive to Alton. It won't hurt to have a half-hour to spare. After you get her back, take the rest of the day off, if there is any, and thanks!"

"Sure thing, Sir. The reports I'm working on now will keep till later. Would you please tell me your wife's name? I can get the address from the files."

"Her name is Susie, but better if you call her Mrs. the Buick is brand new, a gift from my Dad, so do drive extra carefully."

Any other reason to get out of the orderly room would have had Higgens jumping for the chance. This trip promised to be just a little more pressure than he needed. He fiddled with the small flashlight in his side pocket, and made a mental note to buy extra batteries after lunch.

The Lieutenant's apartment had a one-car wide driveway with only the new two-tone Buick parked to the rear. Higgens parked on the street, and debated whether to move it to the driveway after pulling out the Buick. Mrs. Churchill opened the door at the first ring. She was talking with a lady in the downstairs apartment next to the building's main door.

"Hi, you must be the hardworking clerk my husband speaks so highly of. You can call me Susie."

Higgens was a little slow to speak, he was after all only eighteen, and here were not one, but two fabulously built, beautiful ladies, and the other one was wearing a thin cotton robe that didn't hide much. Mrs. Churchill was wearing a light summer dress. It was tight in the important places.

"Shall we go?" said the Lieutenant's wife; "you

may call me Susie. Would you like me to drive there? I need to go to Tenth Street, across from the Sears store," she said.

"It might be better if I get the feel of the car, so if you don't mind, I'll drive," was his reply.

Driving a jeep, or his beat-up '37 Ford was world's different from the new Buick. Once they started, the Buick responded a bit faster to the accelerator touch than he anticipated. With the jeep blocking his view he had to hit the brakes to keep from backing into a passing car. The brakes also were far more effective to the touch than he was used to. Once her neck stopped whipping, Susie gave him a look that questioned his driving, but she said nothing. That was just the beginning of a very bad drive for Higgens. By the time he reached a light that changed just as he got there, he again hit the brakes too hard, and Susie bounced off the dash but she didn't complain. By now Higgens was sweating so much he could smell his body odor. He concentrated on driving. The downtown section of Alton is all steep hills like a little San Francisco, but by special effort, he had no more problems with the gas or brakes, right up till they reached Tenth Street, and she yelled, "turn here." He spun the wheel too fast, and the lieutenant's wife ended on top of him. After that it took him forever to get the Buick into a parallel parking place. He was so rattled he didn't get out and open the door for her.

She just smiled and said "I may be a good hour.

Here's some change for the parking meter."

He sat; banging his fist on his leg, promising himself the return trip would be better. What if she told the Lieutenant how poorly he drove? He would never head the end of it, when the word spread to his buddies. In a supply depot, there was never much of interest to talk about. On the bulletin board was a sign. "IF YOU DON'T HEAR A RUMOR BY 10:00 O'CLOCK, START ONE!" The car parked ahead of him left, so he inched the Buick to the edge of the white line, giving himself extra room in case he got blocked in tight. That he might dent the Buick was too much to even think about, but that it never left his thoughts.

Higgens locked the car and went to the waiting room just in case she might need help. It was good he did; when she came out a nurse was helping her.

It's good she brought someone, she's a little dopey and will be for awhile" the nurse said.

The drive back went much better; it might not have been that she would remember anyway, as she was all but asleep till they reached the apartment. By then, Higgens must have been thinking he was back in the jeep. He hit the brake for a child on a bike that was way down the street and had to grab Susie to prevent her from hitting the dash. When he grabbed her he almost pulled her dress off. She came to, in time to straighten it and gave Higgens another look. At the apartment he helped her up the stairs and into her room when she almost fell. He walked her into the bedroom. She dropped on the bed, and immediately began to take off her dress. Higgens was a bit too slow to move. She turned around and said, "You can go now," in a very firm voice. He was halfway down the stairs when she called him back.

"I forgot to thank you. How you drove the Buick will just be our little secret. Tell my husband that everything was fine."

It was almost four, and while his Lieutenant said he could take the rest of the day off, he went straight back to his desk. Higgens was so glad to have this duty; he never missed a chance to prove how much the company needed him. The sergeant that was the Company clerk was a career old-timer with a drinking problem. He was more than willing to let Higgens do most of the work. All Armies generate tons of paperwork, but a supply company has many times as much; in fact, that was just about all they did. About the only time Higgens would get yelled at would be for using his flashlight. There was a wartime blackout and if he worked late, he would need to use the light as he walked back to his quarters.

A week had gone by, and it looked like the lieutenant's wife had not said a thing about his poor driving. Then one Saturday as he was having lunch, he got a phone call. It was the Lieutenant's wife. "Hello, Corporal, it's Susie Churchill. I wonder if you could do me a big favor?"

Higgens hesitated, then said, "I guess so. What do you need?"

"My husband is playing golf and I have to be at the General's house for bridge this afternoon. My regular baby sitter can't make it. It would be only for a couple of hours and our little dear will sleep most of the time. I'll pick you up in a-half hour.

Higgens didn't think he had said yes. He tried to worm out. "I've not much experience with babies and was planning to catch up on some rush invoices today. Can't you reach some high school girl?"

"But I'm sure you'll do just fine, you wouldn't want me to forget and tell everyone on the base about your driving, now would you?"

The word "blackmail" was on Higgens lips, however, what came out, after a pause was, "Will one o'clock do? Don't come to my barracks. Pick me up at the newsstand just before the main gate."

"Yes, one o'clock will give me time to carefully go over what you will need to know. The bridge does not start till two."

When Higgens rang the doorbell, it was answered not by Susie Churchill, but the wife of Lieutenant Green who lived in the lower apartment. He explained he was there to baby-sit for the Churchill's. It took a good forty minutes for Susie to go over just about everything one could think of in the care of babies, and any kind of emergency that might happen. As she left, she said there was soda in the fridge, but best not to touch the beer. She left, but he heard her stop and have a conversation with the lady downstairs. He gave the baby a bottle when it cried an hour later, and in ten minutes it was back asleep. Higgens was almost asleep when the door opened. It was not Susie, but the Lieutenant. "What are you doing here?" he asked.

"Your wife couldn't get a baby sitter, so she called me, is that all right, Sir? She had a bridge game at the Base Commander's house."

"Well, I guess so; I can't take you back and leave the baby alone. Did she drive you here? I don't know why she couldn't get Lieutenant's Green's wife to watch the baby.

"I think she went out just after I got here," said Higgens.

At four, Susie Churchill came back and asked her husband to take Higgens back to the base and give him ten dollars. She had lost all her cash at bridge. Higgens tried to say that the pay wasn't necessary but ended up taking it. He would never have told about the blackmail, but sure wished he could. Higgens had no idea how blackmail worked, how that one time of poor driving would lead to major problems.

The next week there would be a parade and a day off as the base closed down for Veteran's Day. Higgens planned to hitch a ride for some home-cooked food. He was in the chow hall when he was called to the pay phone to take a call.

"Corporal Higgens, this is Peggy Green. You know my husband, Lieutenant Green. We live in the apartment with the Churchill's. I want you to do me a little favor tomorrow after the Parade."

"What kind of favor?"

"Not over the phone. You will meet me at the newsstand in ten minutes." Then she hung up.

What was Higgens to do! He hardly touched his meat loaf and then gave in, bolted down a few bites and headed for the newsstand.

"Get in the car," demanded Peggy as she leaned over to open the door. She showed more cleavage than Higgens had ever seen. He got in; he did his best effort to be brave and said, "I'm sorry, but you are wasting your time, I've already made plans for tomorrow."

"Listen, you little twerp, how would you like to spend the rest of the War in a dark dirty stockade cell in Leavenworth, Kansas? I have you by the balls and you know it."

"What are you talking about?" Said a very shocked Higgens. Did she say dark, he thought.

"For starters, an enlisted man is not allowed to be alone with an officer's wife, not to mention fooling around. I saw you take a helpless Susie upstairs and you were there too long to be innocent. Then the second time, babysitting, my ass! You were alone forty-five minutes that time."

"You're nuts! I did nothing wrong," said a surprised Higgens.

"Even if you are right, a word from me and, you know, it's off to the front. So can the bullshit while I tell you what you are going to help me with."

Even if she was full of lies, She could cause so much trouble that he could get transferred to a combat outfit; that's what Higgens thought. It was not that he was so afraid of getting shot, but his problem could lead to great danger to him and his buddies. His uncle had drilled into him how most guys really were fighting to keep their buddies alive. She did have him by the balls.

Higgens gave in, he could not take a chance she might do it. She then detailed her strange request. He was to go to St. Louis, pick up a dress at Sticks Department Store, see a movie, and bring the dress and his notes about the movie to the newsstand at six p.m. She gave him some cash and dropped him a few blocks from base. Higgens didn't like what was happening, but he saw no real harm. None of it made sense to him. The movie he saw was called "Four Feathers." It was about English soldiers and courage. The next week, she made him do it again, on Saturday. He saw a double feature, a Western and some Abbot and Costello film.

Higgens made one of his regular phone calls home. The folks were out, but his teenage sister was home. He asked her what she thought about a buddy of his having to shop for a lady, and take notes about a movie. What would that be all about? She asked if it was a married lady.

"Don't you ever listen to any soap operas on radio? The lady is cheating on her husband, she needs to prove she went shopping and was gone for awhile. Boy, are you men dumb!"

For the next three weeks, none of the wives bothered Higgens, and he began to think the blackmail was over, when Peggy Green pulled up to the bus stop as he was heading to town, and ordered him into her car. It was a Friday evening and Higgens was to meet some high school buddies for a trip to the red light district of East St. Louis. "Where are we going?" He asked.

"Count your blessings, kid. You are going to help me with an experiment, no, a testing of a method, an adventure in something wild. You have proved to me that you know how to keep your mouth shut, so just sit back and shut up."

She turned into a motel that was known by the GI's to rent by the hour, or so Higgens had heard. When she went right past the office and parked around back, he said, "don't you need to check in?" She just smiled and waved a key in his face.

In the room she pushed him to sit on the bed and

began to remove her dress.

"Hey, you're not a virgin, are you?"

He said "Hell, no!" in the manliest voice he could. The fact is Higgens was what was called a sober virgin, sex only while half drunk.

"Take off your clothes. This place is not free." She opened a small refrigerator, and took out two beers, opened one and gave him the other. Sitting next to him and wearing a black set of underwear, she outlined what was to happen, to the amazement of Higgens.

"You see, kid, I want to surprise the Lieutenant on his birthday, with some kinky sex. Not the old, flat on the back, but something exciting and I want to try it out first.

As Higgens got down to his shorts, she pulled a ping-pong paddle from her purse, put it in his hand, and draped herself over his lap. "Now hit me, not too hard, till I say stop. It's called flagellant and they do it all the time in England."

Higgens gave some easy whacks. He had never hit a girl before. She cried for more, then had them switch places and pulled his shorts down to show him how hard he was hitting She kept asking him if she was hitting too hard. Then she checked his erection, and declared it must like this as she gave him a few more. He had never been so aroused before, but felt a deep sense of shame. Did married couples always act like this, he thought.

She finished her beer and had them try it without the paddle, just the flat of the hand. Next thing he knew they were both nude and she helped him put on a rubber, the kind the Army gave away. First, she climbed onto him, then rolled over. She was whispering in his ear to "give it to me." To his shock, she started hitting his butt with the paddle in time to his pushing. It was over before he knew it and she arched her back and dumped him on the floor. Before he could get up, she was in the shower and called him to join her. When they got dressed, she stopped him at the door and made him put his hand on the Gideon Bible.

"Now, swear you will never tell anyone about this," she ordered.

"I swear, I'll not tell any of my buddies." When that did not satisfy her, he added, "or anyone in our Company."

"You better not, if you know what is good for you," she said, her face just inches from his. He looked at his watch as she started the car, and was surprised that it was less than an hour since she picked him up.

For the next few days Higgens avoided looking at Lieutenant Green. He worked out a plan to keep this from happening again. He limited his movement to work, the chow hall, and even moved a folding cot into the back of the orderly room, so he couldn't be approached by any of the wives. He also took no phone calls. When he would run out of work, he had his buddies bring him books and magazines. Nevertheless, Mrs. Green caught him coming from buying batteries at the commissary and gave him a note. He was to get her the 201 personnel files on the other two Second Lieutenants. There was a phone number for him to call when he had them. He called and told her he could go to jail for that. He could see she was looking for something to blackmail them with, in hopes of advancing her husband over the other two. She slammed the phone when he said no, after giving him two days, or else.

That night he did not sleep, but at dawn, came up with his only recourse. Higgens went to see a Catholic chaplain on the other side of the base.

"You don't know me and I'm not a Catholic, but if I tell you something in your confessional, can you give me advice, and it's just between us?" He asked.

He saw the fear in the boy's eyes and sensed his need. "Come with me, my office will do. Unless you're a German or Japanese spy, there is nothing that a GI can't tell a chaplain. It's covered by the Uniform code of Military Justice."

Higgens told the whole story of his being blackmailed; leaving some details out and explained he had sworn on a Bible. He also left out the reason he could not be transferred to the Infantry. The Chaplain was a very astute listener, and asked about that part of the problem. Finally in desperation, Higgens opened up.

"It's called achluophobia, fear of the dark. I've had it since I was a kid. I'd scream and have a fit when I was small unless my folks left a light on in my room. We ended up seeing many doctors. They tried psychiatry, the works. Finally, the family doctor said, 'just leave the damn light on till he grows out of it.' But I didn't. So you see, if I was in combat I could get my buddies killed. My dad had our congressman check all the way to Washington. That condition would not get you a 4-F classification. I learned typing and such, so I could stay back in the rear."

"What did you do in basic training, and how do you sleep?" the Chaplain asked.

Higgens pulled out his small flashlight. I pull covers over my head and use this light.

"Don't the batteries run out?" He asked.

"I hold the button that makes it light only when pressed. When I fall asleep, it goes out. Sometimes I wake up while it's still dark and I get it on before the panic starts."

"I'm going to help you, Higgens. Go back to work and wait till you hear from me."

He went straight to Higgens commanding officer, Major William Lynch. "Bill, you trust me, you know I've never lied to you and we both want what's best for the Army."

Before he could say more, the Major cut in, "Get to the point."

The Chaplain took a deep breath, and said, "There is a GI on this base that has come to me with the most unusual problem I have ever had and I believe him. He is in a bind that is not his fault. He is a good, no, a fine young man. It would be a tragedy for his career to be ruined and it will be unless we do something about it. The problem is, I can't tell you what it is. The solution I have in mind is easy and is best for all. Will you help me help the Army and this GI?"

All the Major said was who is it, what is your suggestion, and please tell me something, however vague, that will help me understand what the hell you're getting at.

"Corporal Higgens has a private problem, an off-base problem, he has broken no laws, and there is no one else in your command that is directly involved. I want you to give him an immediate emergency leave, till you can cut orders transferring him to another base. It has to be a non-combat placement as well."

"Hell, is that all. Then again, I'm a little bothered by the non-combat aspect."

"Major, he's not a shirker, there is a true and I believe, a good reason for that part of it."

"Higgens is my best clerk. I would hate to lose him. You sure I can't solve this?" Said the Major. When it was plain to see the Chaplain was waiting for an answer and would not go into more details, the Major gave in. "All right, I believe you, hell, excuse me, you don't even cheat on your golf score. And anyone that plays as poorly as you should. Look here!" He pulled a paper from a pile on his desk; "that kid is in luck. The Army wants to expand the re-supply station at the Presidio in San Francisco, the base we all would like to be at. He can start a one-week emergency leave at 12:00 hours today, then report to Jefferson Barracks in St. Louis till his shipping orders come through. I'll miss him. Hell, Higgens even works nights. Who else around here has that kind of attitude?"

While a surprised Higgens was at home, Peggy, the wife of Lieutenant Green, was in a motel room spanking the butt of the base commander and giving him such wild sex, that her lieutenant was granted a promotion to First Lieutenant and a transfer to the base of his choice. He chose the Presidio in San Francisco, California.

THE END

AWOL

"Major Labbs will see you now," Susie said, with her usual fake smile.

"This had better be good; you've had more leave than any man in this outfit has. I'll give you thirty seconds to convince me," said the Major.

Sergeant Howard Hale was trying to get a leave. He had already used up all his leave time and then some. His request for an emergency leave had just been turned down.

"You see, sir, the lady was like a mother to me, I lived three houses from her, and she was a widow. My cousin and I called her Aunt Alice and took care of her. I have this letter from her lawyer. She died on Monday, and has left her estate to my cousin George and me. If I leave today, I can make the funeral. My cousin, George is not the kind of guy you can trust. I don't want to be cheated out of any money. Sir, I can retire in just two years and am saving to buy a boat yard. So yes, it is an emergency. I only need a few days."

"The book is quite clear. She is not a blood relative. Leave denied! Get a lawyer back there in Ohio. Dismissed!"

"It's Iowa, not Ohio" Hale whispered under his

breath as he left the Major's office, and gave Susie a big fake smile and the finger, but behind his back where she could not see. There was a story about her getting mad at some guy who made a pass at her. His pay records got lost twice.

Hale found his friend, Tom, an MP, having a cup of coffee at the Base Exchange cafeteria. "I can tell by your long face that the Major turned you down. Serves you right, you have had more leave this year than anyone I know has. I mean, hell, you even had a basket leave the Major does not know about."

If I have to wait months, my cousin George will find a way to strip the house. Hell, he might even sell the house and all that land."

"How much land is there? It may be worth more than the house." asked Tom, the MP."

"I think it's about four acres, and right in town next to the creek. I know she had offers to sell it, but was holding on to it in case her daughter was moving back. That girl moved away as soon as she could and never came back as far as I know, and she died last year. Aunt Alice only had that one girl. There was no other family, so I'm not surprised she left George and me her estate. When I sell my half, that plus what I've saved should be all I need to buy the boat yard I have my eye on. But how do I keep George from ripping me off?"

"Whatever you do, don't even think about going

AWOL," said Tom, his MP friend. "You know what happens when you take that route!"

"Sure do" said Hale. "They call your hometown police, you're locked up, there is no bail, and when they send for you, it's an MP and one noncom from your outfit. The cost of their and your travel is taken from your pay. What is it, they only have to travel 500 miles a day, then they can stay at a good hotel and eat at your expense?"

"The rules are not clear; the pickup crew doesn't have to go over 500 miles a day, but lots of times when they take a train or fly, that doesn't apply. I like to take a train; the club car is better than the one little bottle of booze served on a plane. The price is better, too."

"That's it!" Said Hale. This talk about AWOL just gave me an idea. What if I could pay some guy to go AWOL and I arrange to be a part of the pickup crew. Hell, there must be guys that would do it for, say, two hundred dollars. I could reimburse them for the cost from what I get for the house and land. What do you think?"

"I don't know, first it has to be some dumb private that lives near your place, one that doesn't give a shit about his record. And the big thing is, can he keep his mouth shut. You could be setting yourself up for blackmail. No guy is going to get himself locked up for a measly two bills, better think about five, at least. Can you make sure you will be on the pickup crew sent to get the guy, if you can find one that will go AWOL for a price?"

"Tom, this idea is starting to look better all the time. There are only four of us sergeants that could go if the guy is from my outfit. I can get the other three sergeants to pass; leaving me as the only one that could go. You are right about it has to be a guy that cares not a hoot for his record, one that has been busted a few times. You have files at the MP office. Could we look for such a guy, anywhere's near Des Moines or on the way will do."

Tom, the MP agreed to check his files and meet with Hale at five in front of the chow hall.

"Hale, I got just the right guy, well maybe, Private Bill Wilson has spent more time in the stockade than out. He's also always broke and likes to play cards, at which he's lousy."

The MP then handed Hale a card with Wilson's name and a small photo from a mug sheet.

"Thanks, but what is the "maybe," said Hale.

"This is not a guy you can trust any further than I can throw a tank" replied the MP.

"You better look for him alone, he knows that I'm an MP."

Hale asked some of the GI's from Wilson's barracks, and found Wilson in the parking lot of a bar off base. He was looking at a beat-up Ford with a for-sale sign.

"Hi! You plan to buy it?" Said Hale, as he walked over to Wilson.

"What's it to you, Sergeant," said Wilson, as he looked Hale up and down.

The car had a price of $400 on the for-sale sign.

"You could buy this for $350, I'll bet, and I know how you can earn $400 easy, that's what it is to me," said Hale.

There was no answer at first.

"How about I buy you a beer and we talk."

"What do I have to lose," was Wilson's answer. They went into the bar and Hale directed them to a back booth. Over two beers each, he explained the AWOL deal.

"You want me to go AWOL, get picked up by cops and then get turned over to you? What for?" Asked a skeptical Private Wilson.

"I like the part about paying $400. $500 would be better, but if I'm going over-the-hill, I get to stay away from the cops more than one lousy day, that's for damn sure."

"Let me explain it again; you go AWOL, I arrange to be on the pickup detail, you have to get caught right away, cause I don't get started after you till the police have you. It's only one night in jail. When I get there the police will turn you over to me, and the first thing I do is to take off your handcuffs and let you escape. Two or three days later we meet. Then I take you back to base. I reimburse you for all the Army takes out of your pay. And, Ok, $500 cash. It will be $100 up-front and $400 when we meet after I have turned you loose. You get a free leave and the money to buy this car. See, I have the up-front $100 right here. Maybe the seller will take that as a down payment and you can drive home. Your home is north of Kansas City, which is right on the way to where I have to go. If you need time to think it over, I can only give you an hour or two, 'cause if you chicken out, I'll just have to find another guy."

Wilson needed only the time it took to drink another beer. They shook hands and Wilson pocketed five twenty-dollar bills. Hale watched him walk away and crossed his fingers.

The next morning Hale called the lawyer for Aunt Alice and told him he hoped to be there in two days, and under no circumstances was he to let cousin George visit Alice's house unless the lawyer was with him.

Including Hale, the company had only four sergeants that were eligible to go on pickup duty to return an AWOL enlisted man. Of the three others, the first two that Hale spoke to were not interested in going on what they called chase duty for a GI that would only go as far as Kansas City. Both of them assured Hale that if they were asked, they would beg off and recommend Hale. Sergeant Nelson, the supply sergeant, smelled a rat and demanded that Hale buy him off for fifty bucks. Before the day was over, all three sergeants talked about it at chow, and Hale ended up shelling out two more fiftys. Counting what he gave to Private Wilson, Hale was now $350 in the hole. All he had to do was wait till Wilson was reported as AWOL and Tom; his MP buddy received word from the police that they had Wilson. Twice a day, Hale called the lawyer Labbs, to reinforce that his cousin was not to have any access to Aunt Alice's property till he got there. That happened two days later. A reluctant First Sergeant cut orders sending Hale after the AWOL private. Hale gassed up his car and took off on the three-hour drive to Kansas City.

The police were cooperative in turning Private Wilson over to Hale. Hale assured them that Wilson would be returning that day to their base stockade at Fort Leonard Wood.

"Boy, am I glad to see you" said Wilson. "My car has a bad transmission and I need two hundred dollars to get it fixed."

While driving Wilson to the garage where his car was, Hale learned why Wilson had been so willing to go AWOL; his girl was dating Wilson's best friend.

Hale gave him the two hundred, but with the understanding it was part of the five bills total. He also advised Wilson that since the transmission broke so soon, he should renegotiate the price with the seller. He would get the rest of his money only when he met with Hale in two days. They could meet at the bus station. Wilson talked Hale into making it three days.

Hale knew that Aunt Alice's house was to be locked, so he went straight to the office of Lawyer Labbs. Labbs' secretary said the lawyer was in the middle of an important meeting and Hale would have to make an appointment and there might be an opening in four days. Hale thanked her, headed for the door, then turned and rushed into the inner office.

"Sorry I had to barge in, I have only two days till I must get back to my base. When can you execute the will or whatever you do?"

The lawyer excused himself from the businessman and took Hale to a hallway.

"You are the second one to barge in on me. I just sent George on his way, since you boys are in such a hurry. I gave him the key and told him to make an inventory. Yes, I strictly informed him he was not to take anything from the property till you got here. I'll talk to my secretary and see if we can meet tomorrow right after my lunch hour.

"You gave George a key!" said Hale. "Noon tomorrow is fine" Hale said as he ran for the door, and spun his tires as he drove out of the parking lot.

The front door was locked. There was no car in the driveway. Hale felt relieved till he heard some noises and ran out back. George had his car on the grass, backed up to the backstairs; his arms held several long guns. An old pistol was stuck in his belt.

"I knew you'd rip off all you could get your hands on" said Hale as he looked in the car.

"You got it all wrong! Said George. I'm just moving things to a safe place. You know if guns are left in this empty house, they will be taken. It's a wonder that the house has not been broken into so far. The neighborhood is not the same as when we were kids."

Hale took a quick look at the guns, and began to check the boxes of stuff on the back seat.

"Look" said George. "There are four long guns, two for me and two for you."

He read the angry look on Hale's face. He put a shotgun and a rifle in his truck and handed Hale a rifle and a shotgun that was wrapped in a dirty oily rag. When Hale looked at the two newer guns that George was taking and the two old ones for him, he started to make a fist.

"Okay, here, have this old pistol to make it even" said George.

"It's not just the guns, what else have you taken? Is this your first trip? Have you already moved all you could to your house?" Questioned Hale.

"Look for yourself in the car; these are pots and pans and dishes. It only makes sense for me to take them. I'm getting married soon. What could you do with them in the Army?"

"Let's go look around together" said Hale as he casually put the two long guns and pistol in the trunk of his car.

"What do you think this house and land is worth?" Hale asked of George, as they took turns opening drawers and closet doors.

"I'll make a guess of sixty thousand for the house and more than that for the land. It's zoned for commercial use."

That said, Hale smiled and took a kinder attitude to his cousin George. There was little else of any great value that they found. George explained he had talked to a guy that ran an auction house. He would buy the contents.

"I have his phone number, we can call him to come and look at the stuff in the morning, what'd think? That would be some quick cash."

"Ya, George, go ahead and call him. We could also sell him all the guns and split the cash. It would be fairer than you keeping the new guns and giving me the old broken down ones" said Hale.

The next morning they met with Alan Reynolds from the 'Old Town Auction Barn'.

He appraised the furniture, personal belongings and basement tool shop. He stepped to one side and worked a pocket calculator.

"You boys are in luck! There are a few good antiques like that end table. We would pay you $2300 for the lot and we do the hauling. Sorry, but we don't buy and sell guns. What do you have, anyway?"

"I have a pump shotgun and a 30-06 Winchester. Hale has a double-barreled shotgun, an old lever-action deer rifle and a funny-looking cap and ball pistol. If you don't do guns, what are you asking for?" Said George.

"Just curious, I know guys who buy old guns. Don't think you have anything they would want" replied Mr. Reynolds.

"You should call us as soon as the lawyer says it's legally your property.

"How soon would we get the money?" Asked George.

"After the sale. That would be in, maybe, six or seven weeks. Who gets the check?"

"Make it out to me, I'll send Hale his half," said George.

"I would prefer that you make out two even checks to us. Give me your notes and I'll put my address on it, said Hale, while giving George a stern look; a look that said 'No way, buddy!"

Hale wished he knew something about old guns. He felt that George was getting the better end of the deal, the deer rifle was brown with rust, and on the pistol he saw that it was made in France. Must be a cheap import, he thought. It came to him, with the many thousands of dollars due them, he was being petty about George taking the good guns and dumping the old ones on him. But I don't even hunt, and at this time it might be wise to stay on George's good side.

They had a good lunch at the best restaurant in town, an idea of George's. Hale had to pay most of the bill. George said he would get dinner after they met with the lawyer and went to a realtor and bank. George asked if Hale thought a realtor would make an advance on the sale of the house and land.

At the lawyer's office, the secretary directed the boys to a large conference room. Lawyer Labbs was there as well as Mr. Carl Swingler from the Main

Street Bank.

The lawyer started with a friendly greeting. "Well, young men, the good news is that in spite of it all, you will leave here with at least some cash."

Hale and George looked at each other in total disbelief.

"Let me summarize what the financial situation is on the property of one Alice Markington. I'll start with the mortgage."

"What mortgage?" Said Hale. "I saw Aunt Alice burn her mortgage years ago!

"The reverse mortgage. Your friend Alice had many bills due to the cancer that killed her daughter. Fifteen years ago she took out a reverse mortgage from Mr. Swingler. You do understand that's a lot like a loan that pays you a monthly fee towards the future sale of your property. At the time it was drawn up, this town had two factories, and the house was appraised at eighty thousand. The advance was to reach a total of fifty-five thousand. The bank never goes over a figure that they are sure the property will bring. As of six weeks ago when Alice had her stroke and went into the nursing home, the bank had advanced a total of fifty thousand. Now that both factories have been shut down, due in no small part to overseas competition, the house is reappraised at 60 thousand. And that is mostly because it has a good location and large lot. Under the terms of the reverse mortgage, one that I approved to protect my lifelong friend, Alice Markingham, the bank will buy the house for the price of that mortgage, giving the estate five thousand dollars"

When he paused, Hale said in a loud voice, "What about the land, does it not go with the house? That's a big lot and in town, too."

Alice sold the land to the lumberyard several years ago, not to be used till she no longer lives there. There is one payment of one thousand dollars still due. That makes a total of six thousand on the plus side. In addition, since you boys have made it clear you want to rush this matter, I took the liberty of calling the auction barn. They put an estimate of 2,300 on the house contents towards, which the bank that handles Alice's money for years, will advance you $2,200 and eighty-six dollars left in her savings account, making a positive total of $7,286.00."

Before Hale or George could get a word in, he went on. "On the negative side, there is only the nursing home bill for one month, of $6,040, which when applied to the $7,286, leaves a total of $1246. I have a check for each of you for $623. That, plus what goods you removed from the house are the best I can do for you. You're lucky that Alice and I made a deal for my fees to be paid in advance, or you get even less. To get these checks, you both must sign these papers."

Hale and George looked at each other in disbelief. It looked like George was going to cry. Hale was adding on his fingers what this trip had cost him to Private Wilson. This did not add up to anything but a sad lesson.

Within hours, Hale was trying to find Wilson. He called his MP friend, Tom, who was supposed to be with him, but was really on a visit to his parent's house.

"I can't find Wilson! He did not meet me at the bus station. What do I do?" Cried Hale to his friend.

"How did you make out, you get a bundle of dough?" Asked Tom.

"No, I did not, any idea on finding Wilson? You're the cop."

"Did you try the local jail? He never could stay out of trouble."

"That punk will be in even more trouble if he tries to collect what he thinks I owe him" said Hale.

Wilson was indeed in the local jail and would never make the bail that had been set, after he stuck a knife in the boy that was dating his girl. The police had already notified the Army and was informed that Wilson would be discharged under unfavorable terms as soon as the paperwork could be done.

Hale told all that to Tom, plus the bad news about the inheritance. When they got back to the base, Tom asked to see the old guns.

"Just look at the rust on this old rifle" said Hale.

"That's not rust, it's the color of the gun; they used a brown, not blue coating. Gee, look at this, here, read this, you lucky jerk!"

Tom held the rifle up to Hale's face and pointed to a number 1 of 1000 on the receiver.

"What does that mean?" Asked Hale.

"It means this is one of those rare one in a thousand Winchester rifles, it's worth thousands today. Show me the other guns. The shotgun was still in the dirty, oily rag; it was a sixteen-gauge shotgun.

"Parker double, that's also a collector item, worth a lot" said Tom. "You said there was an old pistol as well?"

Hale took out the clumsy heavy revolver with the French name. "That's a rare LeMat. It was a favorite with the confederate calvary. I have no idea what it's worth. see this fat barrel? It's to load as a shotgun. Keep these under lock and key till I make a few phone calls. What were the guns that your cousin George kept?"

Hale described the 30-06 Model 70, and the

pump shotgun.

"Together, not worth more than six or seven hundred. You got the better part of that deal. George outfoxed himself, taking the newer guns and giving you the old ones."

By the time Hale had reported to the Major how Wilson had escaped from him and had a big time ass chewing, Tom had located the value of the old guns, a total of $66,000.

More than enough for Hale to buy the boat works when he retired.

All for raking some leaves and being nice to a little old lady, Hale thought. He resisted the urge to tell Cousin George about the guns.

Hale began to start counting the days till his discharge.

THE END

HAZEL THE JEEP

On the wall behind the bar in a tavern in Brooklyn is an eight by ten framed black and white picture. To the left of the picture is a worn one-dollar bill with a big number one on it and marked "the first of many." To the right are two ten-dollar bills taped together and covered with names written with fountain pen ink, many unreadable. GI's would know this as a "short shorter." Three of those names were on the picture. It was a photo of a WWII jeep with three young Army soldiers standing in front and a sergeant sitting at the wheel. Inside the frame covering the back half of the jeep hangs a Purple Heart medal. I asked the bartender about the picture and learned the owner is the private on the left. He is now retired and living in Florida during the winters.

"Is that his medal?" I said, referring to the Purple Heart.

"No, it's not his, but that medal goes with the picture."

"Can you tell me about it?" I asked.

"Hazel, the jeep was one very special jeep. Some believe it was magical. I think it was possessed, maybe by the spirit of some Detroit worker killed in an accident. Or maybe just coincidental, but that jeep saved the lives of those guys several times. See the metal poles sticking up from the front of the jeep? Those are machine gun mounts. This was a recon jeep and crew. The sergeant behind the wheel was in charge. I forgot his name and can't read it on the picture. He was in here once and told how the jeep had a bad habit of stalling or making sudden stops. He knew of two times when that saved their lives. Once at a crossroad when it stopped as if out of gas, but the tank was full. Then a minesweeping crew yelled at them, but Hazel, the jeep got a flat and they fell behind the convoy. The plane hit the last truck right where they would have been except for the flat."

"Is this his metal?" I asked. "And where did the name Hazel come from?"

"No, the sergeant was never hit. Hazel was the aunt of Bill, the owner of this place. He said she had a great sense of humor and always looked after him when he lived with her during the first two years after his folks split up."

"The guy in the middle is Tom. See how skinny he is? Well, he was here last New Year's and I'll bet he weighs close to three hundred. He still has a piece of German steel in his leg from the round that destroyed Hazel."

"So it's his medal? I inquired.

"No, his son has his. He lives not far from here and brings his friends in to see the picture and have a beer after ballgames."

"I give up," I declaimed, "and just whose Purple Heart is it?" "Hazel's," said the bartender with a wide smile. "The only jeep to earn a medal."

"How can that be?" I spoke, as he drew me another beer.

"The way Bill tells it, on the breakout called Operation Cobra, just after Normandy, our own Air Force screwed up. Got their directions mixed and started to drop loads on our guys. The recon team and Hazel were right in the thick of it. Bill swears that without any help from the driver, Hazel got them the hell out of there and raced, flat out in the only safe direction. That saved their lives. Soon after the hedgerows were passed, someone missed a German 88 and it started to get the range of our recon crew. All the guys say the driver tried to go left, but Hazel turned right and the next 88 hit in the ground and tore into the jeep's motor. Hazel took the hit that would have got them."

"The next day, Bill handed some busy lieutenant a stack of medal award forms to sign. One was for Private Hazel for a head wound. For a serial number he used Hazel's motor number and listed in very fine print, 'concussion to head gasket' When the medal came, they got a guy from another outfit to say he was Hazel. That's the story they tell. What'd yah think—magic or spirit? I think the medal was not enough. That jeep should be on display at the War College or the Pentagon."

THE END

ERNEST THE CLOWN

Ernest was an Eagle Scout, an A-plus student, president of his church youth group and treasurer of the young Republican's club. And for the last two years, Junior State chess champion. He was at five-foot three, the shortest member of the high school track team. Track was the only sport he ever tried; he held onto fourth place in the one hundred-yard dash. In his time, Ernest was a gold-plated geek. He had four older brothers that pounded on him for as long as he could remember. The only defense Ernest developed was humor. He knew more jokes than anyone did in a high school of over two thousand students. He had also developed great skill at mime.

Many times Ernest got in trouble for mimicking his teachers. He would imitate their voice and mannerism to the delight of other students.

Ernest went to the University of Illinois for the summer after his junior year. He was picked on before he could use humor as a defense. He decided he was not ready for college. When his advisor suggested he might try the service before college, Ernest joined the Air Force after graduation. He just happened to get in a group that had the worst T.I. (Training Instructor) in the entire history of the Air Force. Their relationship was a match made in the bottom of hell.

Airman First Class E-4, O'Connor believed his job demanded that he act mean for at least twenty-four hours a day. He also made a lot of stupid mistakes and was careless in keeping time of the activities of basic training. Then there was the fact that he had the morals of an inner-city rat. He was in the service as an alternative to going to jail. His only attribute was that he was tall and looked like a recruiting poster of a sharp soldier.

When Ernest and sixty-nine basic recruits got off the bus at Lackland AFB in Texas, O'Connor had them form one long line by height. Ernest was at the far end when the T.I. called for anyone with prior military service to step forward. When none moved, he defined his request to include ROTC, National Guard, and even Civil Air Patrol. Ernest had tried the Civil Air Patrol till he got sick on his first and only flight. Seven recruits then took one step forward. The T.I. picked the first six out and said that "thanks to your training you six will be my latrine patrol, taking turns, three each day. You will make sure the barrack's latrine is shipshape." That left Ernest.

"Can you run?" Asked T.I. O'Connor.

"Yes, sir, I was on the track team, Sir." Then Ernest saluted the T.I. as he tried to get off to a good start. There was only one problem. Ernest used a Boy Scout salute. The T.I. screamed a few swear words about where did Ernest think he was. He made Ernest do an about-face and hold the salute so the rest could see. They all laughed till he made them stop.

"You are the chow runner for our squadron. Get back in line you idiot." He then marched them to Barracks Number 105 and pointed out that would be their flight number for the next eight weeks.

During basic training, the mess hall, also called the chow hall, and some days other names not suitable for most civilians, could not be expected to feed thousands of GI's at the same time. The chow runners system evened out the flow. T.I.'s would send their runner about ten minutes ahead to report in to an officer at the mess hall. He would then send them to bring their group as the line moved down. The chow runner got yelled at a lot and was expected to race the runners of other groups. The upside was that he would get a chance to sit and write letters or visit a candy or cigarette machine. This perk made Ernest somewhat popular with his buddies. But his screw-ups also got all of them yelled at. He was blamed for more than was really his fault. O'Connor did not need any reason to give them a hard time, but would use any slip by Ernest as an excuse to play bad guy and take away any of the few small privileges they had. The first time Ernest had to stand guard duty, their lieutenant came in the barracks and Ernest had to call the building to attention and salute. He did it again, the Boy Scout salute and drew a kick in the rear from O'Connor and a lot of razing from his buddies.

On Sunday of the third week of training, they were marched to an outdoor theater for a show by the base band and glee club. While they waited, the T.I.'s grouped in the back to visit and smoke. O'Connor had left his swagger stick in his car and replaced it with a schoolroom hickory pointer. A flight of WAFs took seats below them. These were the first females they had seen since they got off the bus. Someone yelled, "Hey chow runner, go get us some of them!"

Ernest jumped up and began to improvise a mime act. He ran in place, then acted out the picking up and returning with a girl over his shoulder. Next, he went through the motions of undoing her top and using his hand to feel her tits. Then making a face, he held his hand to show they were too small. He dumped her and ran in place to get a second. Then held up his hand with his fingers spread as if holding a grapefruit. And made a big smile. During the last part, a sergeant stepped on the stage and began to outline the show. All the guys around Ernest were so distracted by his mime act that they paid no attention to the stage. That brought T.I. O'Connor on the run. As he tried to get to Ernest, he hit a guy with the stick and the rubber end-cap came off. Then when he reached the row behind Ernest, he whipped the stick at Ernest. He aimed at the collarbone, but Ernest turned his head and was hit on the back of his ear. The stick without the rubber cap had a squared-off sharp end and the result was a bloody mess, as it cut deeply into

Ernest's ear. Ernest screamed and the blood flew. O'Connor then grabbed him by the collar and dragged him out of the crowd as fast a s he could, but not fast enough. The top sergeant had seen the whole incident and called for O'Connor to take Ernest to the base hospital for treatment. It took nine stitches to repair the back of the ear. The next day O'Connor was before the C.O. getting the dressing-out of his life and losing one stripe, equal to a pay cut of thirty percent. And Ernest was transferred to Flight Number 109 which had a T.I. ten times better than O'Connor. Ernest was a kind of hero. No one had ever got a T.I. busted.

The last week of training, as Flight 109 passed T.I. O'Connor, they all turned and saluted him with a Boy Scout salute.

THE END

THE AIRMAN THAT WANTED
TO BE IN THE INFANTRY

While other boys were playing baseball, John was crawling in the deep grass. Other boys held baseball bats; John held a broomstick. It was in his nine-year-old mind a rifle and he was closing in on the British sniper that was about to shoot his dog before it could warn them. Eight years later in 1943, there was no surprise to his parents when John said he wanted to talk with them about his future.

"I'm dropping out of school and joining the army." He stood tall as he made the serious speech he had planned for a week.

"Are you sure?" Questioned his Dad, even while the man's face lit up in a proud smile. "If you finish high school and go to college, you could join as an officer, you know.

He looked to his mother for her reaction.

"Are you going to join the infantry like your father and grandfather?" She asked.

"The recruiter said the Army makes that choice but if I ask, it will help, and most of the Army is infantry. Uncle Lloyd has been teaching me ever since he came home with his leg wound. He has me shooting cans with the .22 as fast as I can and still hit three out of four. He has been showing me how to crawl on my elbows and knees and hide in the grass."

Three days later, June the first, 1943, two days after his seventeenth birthday, his parents' permission papers in hand, John reported. A train took him from their farm town in Illinois to a base in Georgia.

On the rifle range John excelled in spite of his small size. John beat most men running the obstacle course; he loved playing real war games.

The second week of basis training, John was tested and then had to report to the assignment officer.

"Sir, I want to be in the infantry." John blurted out before the startled officer said a word."

"What are you, some kind of wise guy? See that line, just about all of them are going to try and talk me out of putting them in the infantry," said the officer.

"I see that you made expert with both the MI and the carbine. I also see that on your records you were some kind of hotshot at shooting skeet. Tell me about that." (He said the last as a forceful order.)

"Well, Sir, I was a junior state champion at skeet, I hit 99 out of one hundred two times. So you see, I belong in the infantry."

"You belong to the Army. The Army has many needs, with your small size and shooting skill. I'm sending you to the Army Air Corps gunnery school. We need gunners for the B-17 planes. You could be just right for either tail gunner or the belly gunner; it's called the ball turret; it takes a small person."

"But sir, everyone in my family has always been in the infantry. My Uncle Lloyd is with General Patton. When Lloyd was home, he trained me on how to crawl, stay low and shoot fast.

"Son, report back to your company. This session is over; you go to the Air Corps. Dismissed!"

At the gunnery school in Texas, John had a hard time adjusting to the heavy machine gun. His first week, he was bottom of his class. The sergeant accused him of not trying. Two weeks later he got the hang of it and jumped to the top of his whole company. When he jumped from a tower during parachute training, he floated so far from the rest they said he would have to carry his gun next time so he would land in the same country as the rest of his crew.

Standing in line to board the troop ship for England, John looked at the lines of men with new MI rifles, then at the old 38 pistol they gave him. The clerk at the armory apologized for the 38, "We ran out of 45's; maybe you can trade up when you get over there."

One day in chow line, John spoke to an infantryman; the guy broke up laughing. "What I wouldn't give to trade places with you kid, you get clean beds and good meals. I'll be wearing my feet out while you fly overhead. Count your blessings!"

To John's surprise another guy took John aside. "I hear they shoot down the B-17's almost as fast as they can make them. The 8th Air Group loses more men than any division. You better learn to speak German and memorize, *don't shoot, I give up!"*

None of this made John feel better than when he and other replacements reported to his new outfit. All he heard was tales about getting shot down. The men traded horror tales about burning planes and German POW camps. And stories of the few that made successful jumps and avoided capture till Frenchmen helped them get back.

Before he could be assigned to a permanent aircrew and plane, he was a last-minute substitute for a side gunner. The flack and noise was terrifying, but once he went to work it was not a problem. Three times his shooting was so close to German fighters that they veered away from his plane. Then he hit one with two good bursts and others of the crew saw it too and yelled things like, "great shooting" to him. Their plane took two bad hits from anti-aircraft guns, but made it back to base with none of the crew hit. John got sick from the drinks, beer and whiskey they kept buying him and making him drink. The next morning they assigned

him to a new plane, but the captain of the one he
had been on got a change made and he became a
regular member of the crew of a B-17 named
"Leggie Lady." Their plane was being repaired so
John had the day off. He went for a walk to help
shake his hangover and heard gunfire. He soon
found a rifle range where the Rifle Company that
guarded their airstrip could practice. They let him
fire a few rounds and he got to know the Officer in
Charge. He agreed with John that if shot down, his
pistol was of little use, but that was all he could take
on the plane. Somehow John got himself an MI
carbine.

John gave the ground crew chief a bottle of
good Irish whiskey in trade for overlooking a
carbine that John planned to carry on his plane. In a
bar he looked up some of the Army parachute
division and got advice about jumping with a rifle or
carbine. They had many things to tell him and on a
visit to their quarters he got a good compass, a rope
to carry and a special hook that he could hang a
carbine from while jumping with a parachute.

John began to have dreams of his plane shot up
and jumping behind enemy lines. With his carbine
he would protect his buddies. In his dream all made
it out and landed in the same area. At that time in
the war, the air crew on a B-17 could look forward
to going home on leave after 25 missions, but the
Germans were shooting down about one of every
five planes in a year. That added up to about an 80%
chance of not making it home. But John and the

Leggie Lady were still making it back to base after every bomb run. In spite of his skill as a B-17 gunner, John regularly applied for a transfer to the infantry, denied each time.

In June 1944, the Leggie Lady was returning from mission number nineteen when German fighter and flack combines to take out both engines. The crew was ordered to get ready to jump; the pilot called that he would wait till the last minute to give that jump order 'cause they were getting close to our own lines. The jump command came while the plane still had a safe altitude. John was one of the last to jump, as he was busy hooking up his carbine and gear.

With his carbine hanging straight down from the special hook he had put on his shoulder strap, John came down on the edge of a small patch of trees, far to the left of the rest of the crew. Hung up in a tree, he was thankful for the advice he had gotten from the Army. With the twenty-five foot rope he carried, he lowered himself to the ground and ran away from the rifle fire he heard to his right.

He found himself coming out of the woods to an open field of tall grass. Behind him he heard trucks as more Germans came to hunt for the downed aircrew. John crawled on his belly into the field; the last place they might look was in the open field. He lay low till dark and then began to walk slowly towards the distant sound of cannon fire. He refilled his canteen from a ditch and ate the last of his emergency food as he moved towards what he was sure was the American lines.

Moving low, once the sun came up, he crawled on elbows and knees along a stone wall. Ahead were tall hedges where he could hear fighting, but could not see any troops of either side. John stopped to try and see which way to go, when from his left side Germans moved in front of him and began to set up a light machine gun. By the tone of their excited voices and the way they rushed, it looked like Americans were coming that way. He steadied his carbine, and at a mere 50 yards, shot all three of the Germans, then the next two that came carrying extra boxes of machine gun bullets. John ran forward, stopped only to break the machine gun and jumped to the other side of the wall. He came right back, chased by a hail of shots by some GI with a Browning automatic rifle. "Hold your fire!" He yelled, you got a friend on this side."

"Stand so we can see you! Came a reply with a thick southern voice.

"Hell No!" I'm not about to stand and get a Kraut bullet. This is a flyer that just shot up some Germans. Hold your fire damn it!" John swore, for one of the few times in his life. He went over the wall just before a German Tiger tank blew a big hole in it, right where he had been. John found himself and a squad of GI's running back to the hedgerow they had crossed before. When they saw who he was, one private began to lead John back towards their rear.

"Flyboy, you sure are lucky you found us, leave it to the Infantry to get you back to your clean bed and not in a German POW camp.

A walk of a-half mile and he was turned over to a corporal, a crusty old soldier with orders to take John back to one of the trucks that were returning for more supplies.

"Lucky thing for you, our Infantry found you; this is no place for a flyboy," he said as John climbed on a northbound truck. The truck driver looked at John's carbine and said "Good thing the Infantry saved you before you ran into the Germans."

The next day, John was back at his air base where, as one that got shot down and back; he received a three-day pass to town before he had to fly another mission. He withdrew his request to transfer to the Infantry.

THE END

A HOT TURKEY DINNER

"A hot turkey Christmas dinner for all the troops, that's what the order is," said the sergeant. "Of course only the rear units believe it could happen. The front line is too long. Men are dug in all along the top of that ridge looking down on the DMZ. We only have the men and trucks to rotate some of them back to get fed. There are just not enough choppers to fly the hot meal canisters to all of them. By the time it takes the jeep to reach the last of them, some will be lucky just to get food that's not frozen. That's the way it is," said the sergeant.

The captain looked at the sergeant and pointed to the snow that had started to build up on the roof of their dugout bunker. "If it takes jeeps, then have the mess crew get them on their way as soon as the food is cooked. Headquarters will call for a report in the morning. Just once I'd like to say that all of my men had hot food for at least one holiday. We went through the same thing on Thanksgiving. At headquarters, they know how many men we have up front, how difficult it is to keep the planes and jeeps running, yet they order us to see that each man gets a special hot turkey dinner. You know it's impossible. Of course, some of it's just for the press, a news crew back there where it's nice and dry and warm. Bring back as many men as you dare and use the choppers to reach the large groups; then get the men back before the red's observers see how few men we have on the line. Keep me up-to-date. You may go now."

It was Korea, 1954. The war was over, but at a standoff along the 38th parallel where allies, mostly American soldiers, manned a front that reached completely across the country. North Korean and Chinese faced them from the other side of a wide-open space called the demilitarized zone, for short, DMZ. The reds would shell every so often and send patrols to test our resolve. Our GI's felt the strain of always being ready to fight off an attack and living in the cold and muck. At the top of the highest ridge, second platoon Charlie Company manned a bunker and radio observation post. It was the most forward position. Corporal Jim Johnson, called Rebel, since he was from Georgia and his lieutenant, John Redmond, moved from bunker to bunker as he checked on the 28 men in the section.

"Time to check in on the radio operator, said the lieutenant, as he turned them towards the small bunker where the radio was well protected by large rocks. All was quiet on the line and there were no complaints of frozen feet. He was always checking on the feet of his men.

"Think we can catch Sparky sleeping?" He asked corporal. Sparky was the nickname of the radio operation.

"Not likely. Oh, he dozes off, but he's such a light sleeper, he'll hear us coming, just as he can hear the radio and jump right up without missing a call," said the corporal.

To their surprise, Sparky was sound asleep with his head leaning far back on an ammo crate and his mouth wide-open facing straight up. The lieutenant started to shake him, but was stopped by Rebel. By gesture only, Rebel pointed to the wide-open mouth and to an assortment of food items that had been left behind from a package from home. The lieutenant nodded his okay with a grin as Rebel poured a healthy slug of Tabasco sauce into the last few ounces of coffee in a mess cup. Then without any warning, he poured the concoction into the open mouth of the sleeping radio operator. They both jumped back. Unfortunately, the radio could not move. Sparky choked, gagged and spit out a stream all over the front of the radio. The laughter was short-lived as they watched him struggle for air. They began to hit him on the back. Rebel produced a canteen of water that Sparky poured into his mouth and spit out with a flood of wet K-rations and whatever from his last meal. It was such an explosion that before anyone could see the danger; the radio stopped making the steady hum that it did when on standby.

"You trying to kill me?" Were the first words the radio operator screamed out. "Get away from here."

When they did not move, he drew his 45 and

shot into the ground near the corporal's foot. He looked at his watch. "You better hope I can dry this off before the next call. Company headquarters calls every half-hour to make sure we're okay. If I don't answer, there will be hell to pay. Especially if the colonel has to make a trip up here with his chopper and finds there's no problem."

The problem had already started. Since the sound of the 45 caused a few of the nervous new troops to let go a few rounds of fire at the nearest bushes that might hide a gook. They stopped when the lieutenant and corporal yelled at them.

Back at headquarters, the mess sergeant reported to the captain. "I worked it out. I can get hot food to all the troops except for the second platoon in Charlie Company. A jeep will get close, and then they'll have to carry the food canisters the last thousand yards, all uphill. The best I can say is the food will be kind of warm."

"There's a pad near them," said the captain. "Can't you send them food with a chopper?"

"All the choppers are doing that all along the line. If I change the route, those 28 will get hot food and 100 guys don't. It worked out that it just takes too long to move the troops back and forth; but if I try that with all of them, by the time some of the men get their meal, it will be 2 o'clock tomorrow, unless you want to ask the general for the use of his chopper, Sir."

"Sergeant, I would in a minute, if there was a chance, but he is firm. One bird has to be there in case of emergency. As for Charlie Company, at least the cranberry sauce will be good."

The jeeps were just starting to arrive from the mess hall that were delivering hot food to load in the choppers. The general's aide came running to the captain. "Checkpoint 105, -second platoon, Charlie Company has missed a call. They could be overrun. There was a report of shooting in that area. I want you to go and find out. The general says it would be okay to take his bird if there's none other available. He wants you to report back if there's no problem, so that he can go to his dinner."

There were smiles on the mess sergeant and captain as they clamped a hot food canister from the jeep to the side of the helicopter. And even bigger smiles that day as 28 men from the second platoon Charlie Company on the front line got a hot turkey dinner for Christmas.

THE END

THE VERSATILE JEEP

From day one, it was the most common love affair of WWII. The GI's loved the Jeep. Strange as it may seem today, that there could be such affection between man and machine, but the fact is the guys were crazy about this four by four vehicle. Why the GI's cared so much for the value of having a jeep that they even stole them. Not that most GI's considered it stealing. All they were doing was to move a government item from one unit to another.

There is no ignition key in military vehicles, so locking them is not an option. When it became apparent that an empty, unwatched Jeep was fair game, either just to use for a single trip or even to repaint with different unit numbers and make a part of your inventory, it became common practice to remove some vital part when parking a jeep. Small parts that required no tools to change such as the distributor cap or rotor were so often removed that many GI's would go to town with one of them in their pocket, just in case a jeep was needed. One of the most unusual ways to steal a jeep is credited to the 8th Air Force or other units that flew the B-24 Liberator bomber. A B-24 could fit two jeeps in its empty bomb bay. All it took was to find them, roll the jeeps on their side and use the plane's hydraulic bomb lift to snatch two at a time. In some theaters of operations, a MP would be assigned to watch the jeeps near the flight line whenever a B-24 landed on their base that was not their own.

General Patton's troops were chasing the Germans across France as a B-24 named "Sassy Lady" was returning from a mission with empty bomb bays. The pilot changed course and followed a flight of fighters, also bearing back towards England. As he had hoped, the fighters landed at a new forward airfield. He radioed in and requested permission to land. He claimed his plane had trouble with a fuel transfer pump and once on the ground his crew could repair it. He had seen a line of new Jeeps parked close to the runway. Half of his ten-man crew distracted the base ground crew while the others loaded two jeeps in his plane. Soon after takeoff a P-38 fighter pulled dangerously close to his cockpit and with hand jesters suggested he change radio frequencies.

"Hey there, big brother" said the P-38 pilot. "You are just what we need. The Germans have put a pontoon bridge across the river not fifty miles to the East. There are truckloads of Hitler's best about to escape. Can you bomb it?"

"Sorry, but we dropped our last eggs on the rail yards. Why can't you guys take it out, your base is nearby!"

"My flight is out of ammo; by the time we reload and refuel, it will be too late. Can you at least rake it with your 50's?"

Again, the B-24 pilot said no, "We might not have enough fuel to return to our home base." But at that same time the bombardier cut in, "you're in luck, I still have two bombs left, lead the way, P38.

Off the air, there was a heated discussion between the pilot and bombardier as to the idea of dropping the two jeeps on the bridge. The pilot did not want to give up the jeeps. He suggested that maybe with their twin 50's of the nose, belly and tail gunner, they could disable a truck and block the bridge.

"No, that won't do it, they'll just dump the truck over the side. The weight of a jeep is 2,400 pounds. I can hit then, for sure, from about 1,000 feet. With four tons of metal, we can take out that bridge. We have to try; hell there's a war on, you know," were the last words of the bombardier as he began to remove ropes and readjust his bombsight.

"I still think it's crazy," said the pilot as he turned his plane back towards Germany. "Jeeps cost money, ya know."

"I know a guy that had to pay for a jeep, they docked him seven hundred. I read that our bombs cost about a dollar a pound, so there is no great difference. I'll need to be lined up with the bridge. I'd miss coming at it from the side."

"B-24 to P-38 lead on, our gunners will strafe in case the bombs miss, we need to come in low, 1000 feet. At that height we won't see the bridge till the last minute. I'll be counting on you to lead us straight in. I want you just ahead and at 5,000 feet." He hoped at that height the P-38 could not see what their bombs looked like.

The German column of trucks and a few tanks had just started to cross the bridge. Since it was a light bridge, they were spread with only three on the bridge at a time. According to Newton's law, a falling object travels at 32 feet per second till it reaches terminal velocity. The jeeps never reached that speed, only one hundred miles per hour was the estimate of the gunners that watched. One jeep missed. But the second hit dead center; the 2,400-pound jeep broke the bridge in half. The current of the river did the rest to hold the Germans till reloaded fighter planes and Sherman tanks could catch up with them.

"What kind of bomb was that?" Asked the P-38 pilot. "I must be ready for an R & R, 'cause your bomb looked to me a lot like a jeep!"

"Just the usual 1,000 pounders, but both did not arm and go off, the weight was still good enough" replied the B-24 pilot over the laughs of his co-pilot.

"Years later, it was learned that German Army Intelligence had spent days trying to understand what "Jeep" meant as a code word for type of bomb.

THE END

FOOL'S GOLD

It was nearly three years since I had found the Fool's Gold. Still too early to tell anyone, but I did tell, to my regret. I told about the Fool's Gold on a long flight from Rome, New York to the air base at Yuma, Arizona. Our squadron from Griffith Air Force Base was being sent down to Yuma, Arizona for rocket training, and on the C-119 National Guard flight, there was not much to do other than talk to each other.

Airman First Class Yakinsky was in charge of our group, and it was he who started the contest. He started right after he used what was called the relief tube, that funnel and piece of pipe that is used as a urinal on military aircraft.

He said, "You know, you guys, how about a contest about the meanest thing we ever did. This relief tube reminds me of the time when I was in the National Guard and we were at bivouac, camped out in these wall tents. We were told that we had to use the regular latrine. Nobody could just step outside their tent and let fly, because there were some women officers that might be on guard duty.

"Well, we had this fat kid; he was kind of a pain in the rear. So he got himself a tin can and he used the tin can and reached outside and dumped it. Well, after he woke us up the first night, the second night

104

I took my C-ration can opener and made a couple of small holes in the bottom of his can. In the middle of the night he got up and was cussing and swearing away and I asked what's wrong. He says, 'I can't seem to hit the can. This is running down my leg and it's cold.' We all laughed so hard! Next morning I threw away his can and I still don't think he knows what happened. Okay, now who can top that story?"

Well, Bill jumped in at the opportunity to kill some time. "No, Sir man Yakinsky," he said. "You may be in charge and a good man, but you don't know what mean is. Now, you think that's mean; that reminds me of a similar story.

"When I was in high school, I was just a sophomore, and this snotty-nosed girl friend of my sister and her buddies put together this Halloween party at our house. I learned from my brother that at midnight they were going to turn off the lights and a ghost would appear. Well, I was sitting on a barstool next to this good-looking blonde who had great buns. My brother told me he was about to turn off the lights. Well, I was going to grab this blonde and plant one on her, when I got this idea.

'I had these rabbit fur-lined gloves. I turned one of them inside out and hid it in my shirt. Then when the lights went out, I put on the glove and grabbed this blonde by the neck and growled. Boy, did she scream. She not only screamed, she wet her pants. She had on white tights and when the lights came back on, was she mad, oh, let me tell you!"

"Okay, now who can top that?"

The next guy to speak up was old Tom from East St. Louis who had survived from a tough town and had no hesitancy.

Tom says, "Yeah, well, you know when I was in high school we had this crazy old English teacher. She was making all of us get up and learn Shakespeare. We had to go to the front of the class and repeat this speech from Hamlet. You know, the one where he goes on about 'To Be or Not To Be'. Well, there was this kid named Bill Jason, I mean, he was a hood, I mean like a gangster.

"When it was Bill's turn to get up in front of the class, I put a sign on his back. The sign said, 'I am a bed wetter.' The class roared. Then when the teacher got us quiet and he was starting to talk while he was saying, 'To Be or Not To Be,' all of us in the back row were saying, 'To Pee or Not To Pee, that is the Question.'

"When we got sent to the principal's office he had the other boys in the back row go to detention. Then he said to me, 'I'm not going to punish you, Jason is going to kill you."

Now it was my turn. Before I could start, we had to move from our part of the plane. Someone had to use the honey bucket, that bag of reinforced paper that served as a toilet for solid waste on those types of planes. Sadly, the smell was at our end of the plane. So to take my mind off of it, I joined in Yakinsky's game. I started to tell them my story about the Fool's Gold.

"You see, guys," I said, "When I was stationed in Denver, we used to go gold panning and rock climbing. And there, one time in the Rocky Mountains in an old cave, I found a great abundance of iron pyrite. You know its called Fool's gold. It looks like gold, but it isn't. My buddies thought I was nuts because I was laughing and digging it out, but there were big beautiful samples and I knew I would find a use for them. Sure enough, I did.

"A few days later, we were on the other side of the base and I saw that some poor airmen had to dig this long drainage ditch along the edge of the ball field. Well, that night, I put the Fool's Gold in one side of that ditch, kind of stuck in the dirt like it was a vein. Then I took a pole and made a few holes a couple of feet back and dropped down some pieces and covered them over. For two days I waited and I didn't hear a thing about any gold strike, so I walked over there.

"Well, where that ditch had been, now there was a huge hole. I mean, you could have put a pickup truck in that hole. Some dumb schmucks had really dug looking for that gold, and there was no pile of dirt alongside the hole. They had hauled all that dirt away to pan it out for gold. All right, so what do you think of that?" What's the matter Yakinsky? You seem to be turning pale, you getting airsick?"

I turned and then Yakinsky got up and suddenly I saw his fists double up.

"You SOB!" He cried, "I dug all night. I got blisters. I thought we were rich."

And then I realized he was the one that had dug up the Fool's Gold. Everybody laughed except Yakinsky. But he did smile and he was still smiling as he pointed to the rapidly filling honey bucket.

He says, "Well, Bert, I'm still in charge and we still got eight hours to fly. Guess whom I'm going to assign to carry out and empty out that honey bucket?"

THE END

MESS HALL 102, KOREA

Sergeant Frank Hooper was handing out some leftover bread to a small group of Korean street children, when a jeep pulled up.

"Hey, Sarg, you about to close?" Asked the driver.

"Yes, any minute now, do you need something? I might have a little coffee."

Sergeant Hooper was far more accommodating than the traditional image of a mess sergeant. Mess Hall 102, called the chow hall by most, was the nearest to the front in this part of South Korea.

"No, I got fed, but you should know there is a recon patrol of limeys a half mile down the road. They asked if I would tell you not to close till they get here. The officer said they had not been properly fed in three days.

"What makes them think they'll ever get *properly fed* in this war?" Replied Sergeant Hooper.

"Their timing is bad, I am closing and hell, I don't have much. How come they are walking. I saw a truck come up from that road not twenty minutes ago."

"Get this," the jeep driver said; "do you know

that tall guy from Texas, the one that wears the big hat? He would only go just so near to the fighting. He made them Brits walk cause he's afraid of getting captured by the reds and brainwashed."

"I know him, he should be afraid; you could brainwash him with a damp cloth," joked the Mess Sergeant. He looked down the road and saw the British soldiers dragging their feet. He could tell even at a distance that they were tired, he could be sure they would also be hungry. What am I to do, he thought. He left the door open and headed for the kitchen food locker.

The British officer boldly walked back into the kitchen.

"I say, sergeant, we're in a bit of a spot, it will be dark long before we could reach our unit messing facilities, could you be so kind as to feed me and my six men? They have been three days on the line with nothing much to chew on."

Sergeant Hooper shook his head. "Have them wash up and take a seat, I'll do what I can, it's late, you know!"

Hooper looked around. He wished he had not let all his staff go so early. They went to a USO show. He did a quick inventory and made a plan. Four cans of Spam were opened, sliced thick and dumped on the grill over a restarted gas stove. He opened several boxes of C & K rations. Into the beef stew and lima beans he added chopped up fried Spam. He had no bread, so he put out a tray of stale crackers. The last touch was from the K rations. He took all the fruit cocktail and poured some old cream over it.

"Here you are, dig in," he said, and moved to the back, looking for some tea bags, but he never found them.

It didn't take the British soldiers long to wolf down the chow.

"I say," said the officer, as he touched the rim of his cap with a baton. Is it your President's birthday today?"

"No, why do you think that?" Returned a curious Hooper.

"In England, the troops always get special food on the Queen's birthday, and I just supposed that the magnificent meal you prepared for my boys was for that reason."

He turned and marched his men out into the now darkening night, and Hooper could hear them singing and cheerfully marching away.

Next day, when he told his buddies what the English officer had said, he never could figure out if the English army food was that bad, Or was he getting a dose of English sarcasm.

THE END

STONE BEAR

"Try talking to the Indian at the end of the bar. If he wants, he can tell how he shot the balls off the Japs." So said the bartender.

In his faded Levi jacket, he looked more like a bum than a fighting man did. His head was turned to the TV, and the back of his neck looked as dark as his worn black baseball cap.

"Can I buy you a beer?" I asked. "I'm Ed Louis, stationed at the air base, but you could guess that."

When he turned to face me, I saw the high cheekbones that pushed out as the only smooth part of a face that looked like the old saddle leather you see in a museum. His eyes were dark, but had the brightness of a teenager's, extremely alert, yet friendly.

"Budweiser —bottle. You that young man writing down the old-timers' war stories," he said, not as a question, but as a fact.

"Marines. Shot a few damn Japs in the Philippines. What were you doing with those MI rifles? I don't know of any parade."

"My buddies and I are part of an honor guard. We had a funeral that ended too soon, and we needed a place to hide, rather than go back to base during the middle of a big inspection. It ended up with a lot of WWII vets buying beer for listening to their old war stories. That gave me an idea for my college writing class. So I keep coming back."

"The bartender said you shot the balls off Japs. Were you a machine gunner?"

"No, not a machine gunner. I did shoot the balls off some of the damn Japs, and with a .22 rifle. They all thought I was crazy, going into the jungle to fight the damn Japs with that little Browning .22. Word got to our CO and we had quite a talk."

Spring 1942 at 4th Marine Headquarters

"Sergeant Grimm, I know you don't want to surrender—hell, no one does—but just how long do you think you'll last out there with that puny popgun?" The Lieutenant Colonel went to the window and tried to get in a little bit more air. It was his way of giving you time to think before responding to his questions."

"It was a hot spring on Corregidor in the Philippines. Food, ammunition, medicine— everything but Japs—was in short supply. No one was coming to our aid.

"Sir, on my own without supplies, I can't carry all the ammo I'd need, but a box of fifty rounds of .22's weighs less than one clip of .30 ball. You know that a .22 in the head will work, and in the jungle, all the fighting is fifty yards or less. The little Browning is a semi-auto, dependable and light. Then there is the one great reason. I'd have thought you would have figured it out."

Now, it was my turn to pause. When there was no response from the CO, I reached into my back pocket and pulled out what looked like a piece of pipe.

"What the hell is that?" Asked the CO.

"It's a silencer, Sir. I got a machine shop mate to make it for me. The .22 is the only gun that you can equip with a silencer that will really work. If the Japs can't see me and can't hear where my shots are coming from, my chances will be a lot better than in a Jap-run POW camp.

"Last summer I was in China. I saw how brutal the Japs are. They bayonet all wounded, and what few POW's they take are starved to death. And in some cases, they cut off heads with those long swords. In one place there were so many heads, it looked like the Japs made a contest of beheading the captured Chinese soldiers. Give me the jungle anytime."

"Sergeant Grimm, you know the 4th Division has no real say. We are assigned to the Army. MacArthur wants us to hold out as long as possible. The Navy, thanks to the screw-up at Pearl Harbor, has no ships to take us off or even bring supplies. Within weeks, we'll be chased off Luzon and dug in on Bataan. You should go while you can—take some of those Filipino scouts you trained with you. Good luck, Marine."

The Lieutenant Colonel stood, saluted, and waved me away, turning to look out the window before I could react.

The Indian took a sip of beer, set his bottle down, and looked at my pad and pen. "Kid, don't take notes. The tale I have for you is true and I don't care what you do with it. But since you will pass it on, it should be in your words. Try to remember what I say and make notes later. Also, there is another reason I'll maybe explain later, but I don't want people seeing me going over this stuff and you writing it down like a damn reporter, OK?"

I nodded and put the pad away. He began to speak as if I was not even there.

"I made a list of what I would need, and with help, began to put my kit together. With a rainproof rubberized sheet, I made a carrying case for the .22 Browning, then with part of a bike inner tube— a waterproof holder for the shells—ten boxes of fifty shells—I made a light hammock from a piece of parachute and bundled up some mosquito netting scraps of the camouflage net used over the artillery. I made a small saw blade so I could put a wood handle on it later. It was not easy, but I rounded up all the quinine and Atabrine pills I could. I traded for a very small set of field glasses; they looked like the kind used at an opera. Some first-aid supplies; sewing needles; thread; fish hooks; oil; a .22-size cleaning kit plus a good Zippo was all that I felt I would need. I began to stockpile some dry food and lots of salt, and packed them with my mess kit and two good canteens. I found some colored grease paint a USO troop had left and made up some small bottles to use as camouflage, like war paint for my face.

"For a test of the .22 silencer, I took one of my best Filipino scouts with me toward the Jap lines, just before dark. On their far right flank was a machine gun and crew. We crawled to within about thirty yards and I told my scout he was to fire only if absolutely necessary. My first shot got the gunner in the forehead; next, his loader in the temple as he turned to see why the gunner dropped; and the third when he looked where the shots were coming from and turned to run—he got it in the back of the neck. No other Japs came, so we took their guns and ammo and slipped back to our lines. Getting those guns made me feel better about leaving my guys. Now it was just a matter of picking the right night and route to get beyond the Japs. I studied the headquarters' maps each day."

The Indian paused for a drink and said "you sure you want to hear all this war bullshit from an old drunk Indian?"

"You don't look drunk to me, and yes, I do," was my reply. I was not sure why he had stopped, but I wanted to keep him going. So I asked, "What tribe are you?"

"My dad is Navaho, and my mother is Cherokee. I grew up on reservations. We were given Christian names, but at home used our real Indian names."

"So you are a real full blood. What is your Indian name?" I asked, and then regretted how stupid I sounded. I didn't want to get too personal.

"I am called Stone Bear. To the BIA, I'm full blood. But really, a long way back, my mother had a white man as a grandfather, great, great, or so. While we know a lot about him, I don't think anyone ever used his Christian name. He was called the White Cherokee. He came to America from Ireland on a bucket. Around many winter campfires his story was told."

`"I've heard some of those ships that came from Ireland were real buckets, hardly safe to make the trip," I said.

Stone Bear, as I now thought of him, must have seen my eyes light up, for after a sip of his second beer, he looked across the bar at nothing and began to speak in a voice that made me feel like he was discussing the Holy Grail.

"No, not a rust bucket of a ship, but he did come

to land on a wooden bucket. In his home he was known as a great hunter and catcher of game animals. He was so good that the English who ruled there called him a poacher. He was standing with an old man when they came with papers telling the old man to tear down his stone walls so the English could ride there as they chased the fox. The stone wall had been made just for that reason. It was hard to grow food when horses and packs of dogs ran there. The man was so mad he threw a rock as the officials rode off. The stone made one of the men fall, and his head hit a rock and he died. Later they said the old man was not so strong to throw a rock that hard. It must have been the White Cherokee.

"He had to get away or be hung. At a nearby fishing town, he let the English Navy take him to help on a ship. He did not know ships, so he had to help the cook. He was not let off the ship near any land, as they feared he might get away. Then one day he saw that when he dropped a bucket on a line to get water, if the bucket fell upside down, it would float. One night the ship got within a half mile of land, and he could see fires on the shore. He went over the back of the ship with a rope and bucket. This was a very brave thing, as he was not a good swimmer. There was an open window to the captain's room and so White Cherokee went in and got a flint-lock pistol and a small bag of gold coins that he felt they owed him for a year's work. In the water he let the bucket hold him up till the ship was gone, and the waves took him to shore. He had a gun, but no powder or even a knife. He walked a far distance, caught small game and made a knife from the metal bands of the bucket. He made fire with the flintlock pistol.

"A farmer gave him a ride to a town where he used the gold to get a horse, a rifle, a shotgun and two blankets. It is told that he was first called by the name 'Two Blankets.' He traveled north and west to get away from the English and any local law that might want a reward.

"In the woods he found an empty Cherokee village where there was only an old man and his wife. Both were sick with the pox. The White Cherokee had the pox as a child and was not afraid of it. He shot them a deer and helped them get water and firewood. When he left a large hunting party of Cherokee braves stopped him. They said that they had been watching him and were planning to take his horse and guns. But he had strong medicine to face the pox and his heart was good to help the old man. They asked if he would like to join them; they, too, were going west. They went to a place where some of the Cherokee's were taking on the white man's ways and building a town with houses. He joined them and in time, took a young Cherokee girl for a wife. She lived there and had many children. I think he came from Ireland about the time of the War of 1812, because two of his daughters made the Trail of Tears, and that was in 1838. I think I got some of the old white Irishman's blood in me, because I can hold my liquor and most Indians can't. I'll out drink any Indian and most white men."

I could see a tear in Stone Bear's eye as he finished his story.

I don't know if I should say anything or just wait for him to start again. After a long pause, I suggested another beer and asked a question. "How did you get to be in the Marines on Corregidor? I thought that was all Army, under MacArthur and Wainwright." I dropped General Wainwright's name, just to let him know I knew my history.

"I was in the Army first, joined up for three years in '19 and '27 when I was just seventeen. It was join the Army or go to jail for something I did not do. I was an Indian and was with a few boys when one got drunk and hurt an important white college boy in a fight. After the Army, I was a reservation policeman till 1938, when the Bureau of Indian Affairs cut our funding. We had to cut back two more men of a staff that had been cut to the bone. This was during the depression, you know. I had seniority but my younger brother was the next to last hired. I made a deal that I would leave and join the Army and my brother would help support my wife and mother.

"Did I tell you, my father had worked as a tracker with the great tracker and outlaw Tom Horn? My father and grandfather taught me many of the skills about tracking and living in the wild."

He stopped, took another sip of beer, looked to see if I was still listening and jumped back in his history. I had to ask, "But you said Army, and yet you say you were a marine?"

"During the depression, many out-of-work men tried to join up. The Army would only think about taking me because I had been in before. The Army officer I finally met after a long wait had such a bad attitude about Indians that I walked out on him and joined the Marines. This time I brought with me proof that I was an expert with a rifle and had been a marksmanship instructor. At the Marine camp in California, I was a rifle instructor."

Stone Bear smiled as he drank beer and looked off toward the blank wall.

"One day at the rifle range, they gave me some men—a small group to train. They had all missed the first training because of being AWOL or sick— not a good bunch of recruits. I overheard one wise-ass remark to the others, 'What the hell—an Indian for an instructor? Are we here to learn bows and arrows?'

"When I learned that he had never held anything but a BB gun, I decided to teach him a lesson. We had Krag 30 06 light carbines to use. I told him, 'That gun is going to kick; hold it an inch from your shoulder.' The damn fool did. That made it kick the hell out of him. Then he swore at me. I would not let him stop shooting till he got five in the black.

Believe it or not, at the end of training, he made sharpshooter and told his TI, 'I learned the hard way from the Indian.'

"The 4th Marine Division was in China. I was just a rifleman giving cover to the engineers who were helping the Army of China, which was getting the hell kicked out of it by the damn Japs. We were at Luzon in the Phillipines waiting for a ship to go back to Pearl, when the war started. We were then attached to the Army"

I noticed that he never called them Japs, but always damn Japs. He must have had a reason—could it have anything to do with shooting them in the balls? I had to ask. "Sergeant, should I call you Grimm or Stone Bear?" I asked.

"I am Sergeant Grimm, first name Tom, like in Tom Horn, but when in the wild or on the reservation, I think of myself as Stone Bear. You can buy me another beer and call me Tom if you like."

I called for two beers and got to the question that had started all this. "Tell me about shooting Japs in the balls," I said.

"It was not hate or meanness, not that the damn Japs deserved anything less, but out of a need to stay alive—well, at first. I had shot many Japs, always one or two at a time, ones that got too far from their support. In guerrilla war, you hit and run or hide. I had sewn parts of the camouflage net on

122

my uniform, and would stick leaves and palm branches on myself and in my hat. I was very hard to see if I did not move.

"Once I could see only three Japs. They were moving toward me, but as I shot the third between the eyes, like the first two, a fourth appeared and he had his rifle up, pulled tight to his face, ready to fire as he moved it around trying to find me. His helmet was down low, and I had no good head shot. He saw me and was taking aim, so I shot him in the balls. You see, a .22 in the heart most likely would have killed him, but not before he could get off a shot. Hit in the balls, he went down like a rock. Then up close, I put one in the back of his head. This was three months after the fall of Bataan and the death march.

"I had been keeping track of one of the camps and had helped some escape to join the Filipino guerrillas. A few days with them and I knew I was a lot better off on my own. Their leaders did not listen and kept going after damn Japs when they were up against too many or had not done good recon. Several times men wanted to join me, but I knew it was better if I fought alone. Half my time was spent getting food and hiding from Jap patrols.

"You like to read?" He asked. "That was the only thing I missed when I was out there. I would read any book I could find. Once I had a half of the Bible, the Old Testament half. I gave it away; it was too violent for me."

That should have sounded funny to me, except Stone Bear was not like any Marine I had ever met. He was a bit on the small size and he had none of the usual gung-ho swagger or blustering air like many Marines.

"Yes, I read a lot," I replied. "In the city, the library was a safe place. My mom writes children's stories. Dad works for a big insurance company. I just did not want to spend two years in the mud, drafted by the Army, so I joined the Air Force. A bunch of us take college courses at the downtown extension. Most of the classes did not appeal to me. The writing class sounded like more fun. So here I am. Want another beer?"

Stone bear held up a half-full bottle and shook his head, indicating a no.

"You ever read Shakespeare?" He asked.

"Yes" I said. "I liked *Hamlet* the best."

He grinned, drained his beer, waved for a refill and waved off my efforts to buy.

"But you want to hear about the damn Japs, so ask away."

By now I had seen the light. I was in the presence of a real natural storyteller, the kind who likes to hear the same story again and again. Unlike most of that kind, he had some real dandy tales. I realized all I had to do was ask an occasional question and keep up the flow of beer.

"Were there other Japs you shot in the balls?" I asked. "And how did you live—did you have others to talk to?"

"I was not alone. There were many Filipinos; some I saw a lot. Joseph helped me a lot. He had a cousin who delivered food to the big camp. So then, I could get word of what was going on. It was bad. The damn Japs were killing the POW's. There were beatings and lack of food, water and medical supplies. Many of the guards were lower class, and sadistic as all hell. I wanted to help them but there was not much I could do. What I could do was try to give the damn Japs a dose of their medicine. I would hunt them. After I had shot several, they beefed up the size of their patrols to as many as a hundred. It made no difference to me. Sooner or later, one or two—mostly two, as they were afraid to go off alone—would get too far from the rest of the patrol. I could pick them off and wait to see when they were missed and which way the rest went. They were so damn scared that they left their own men, not even checking to see if they were dead yet.

"I used to know the Japanese words, but have forgotten. At first, they called me the Unseen Enemy. Later, they knew me as Shadow Demon. That was, by the way, how I got most of my food. Either the Japs had some rations in their backpacks, or I would trade with the guerrilla band or the natives for rice and other food. I gave the guns,

125

ammo, and shoes to the guerrillas, but not the bayonets. The natives like to make them into Bolo knives.

"When I ambushed the damn Japs, they were so sure I was shooting from a long way off that they charged right past me and spread out about two or three hundred yards away. I would be right under their noses, twenty to thirty yards or less, holding very still, wearing a lot of jungle. I learned from Joseph that they were puzzled about the reason I would sometimes cut off the pant legs of a dead Jap. Joseph asked me about it many times, but I would not say.

"Joseph asked me if I would dare shoot one of the guards right in the camp. There was one really bad guard; they called him Rat Face, or Rat Jap. He was the worst; always kicking the prisoners if they did not bow low to suit him. Because of the lack of food and medicine, a man that got beaten would die from infection in the open wounds. It was a request from some of the men that they would draw lots and one of the weak that knew he had little chance of making it would get Rat Jap near the fence where the brush is only fifty yards away. It could be done just before dark.

"I said I would try, but during a hard rain would be better. We set a signal so they would know I was there, and likewise, so I would know when they were going to try. Joseph came back a week later to say waiting for the rain was not working—Rat Jap

126

was getting worse. So I went just before dark. I really went during the night before and spent the whole day covered with brush. What I saw made me determined to shoot Rat Jap and a few others. The brave volunteer did not bow, and Rat Jap knocked him down and began kicking him with heavy boots. I was dying to shoot, but the damn Jap did not give me a good target. Then, since I was tired of looking at his backside, I shot him in the balls, then in the gut, as I wanted him to die slow. I was gone a mile before they even knew he had been shot. The .22 made such a small hole and he passed out from the pain; they must have thought it was a heart attack. It was bad, for I learned they executed the volunteer and the other ten that bunked with him. The shot in the balls had a terrific psychological effect on the damn Japs. Joseph said that the Jap commander had a steel jockstrap made for him."

"Tom," I said, "were you always hungry? What was your diet like?"

"You would never believe it, but I gained weight," he replied. "You see, from December 8th till the surrender in June, we were on half rations and less. I would cook rice in my canteen cup. That's a big metal cup that fits under the canteen, and it holds a good quart. I'd shoot a bird or small animal and cook that over an open fire in the mess kit or in a Jap helmet. I also got a lot of a kind of sweet potato. Many small villages were abandoned because of the Japs. I could dig the sweet potatoes and sometimes catch a pig that had gone wild.

"One time I caught a small pig and was taking it back in the woods where the people of that village had hidden out, when I shot another damn Jap in the balls. He and two others were about to rape a girl who had been washing at a stream when I ran into them. I shot the first two before they knew what hit them and the last as he tried to run away. The girl had tripped him, and I was so mad that I first shot his balls as he lay on his back and tried to get a pistol out. I even cut his balls off and wrapped them in one of his socks. That led to a funny thing. After I stayed with that village a few days, I moved on and found myself in a bad place. I was moving up a ridge late in the day when a big patrol of damn Japs came up from my right. All I could do was hide in a bunch of bamboo. One of the damn Japs stopped and sat down right next to me. He had a food pack on his back and I slowly got out the rag of Jap balls. And as he got up, I slipped the balls into his pack. I would have given a lot to be there when that bunch sat down to eat.

"That was one of the few times I shot any in the balls. Most of the time it was in the head.

"Once, I came down with malaria. I had no quinine or Atabrine. I just made it to a village of the pgymy tribe. I had helped them many times. They had herbs that worked, and while there, I learned a lot about the different herbs. There was one that was a great laxative. It was the bark of a strange tree. You had to use only a small pinch to do the job. There were others for tropical diseases. I took a good-sized collection with me."

"How did you cook your food and not have the smoke and fire give your positon away?" I asked.

"I cooked at night or in places where I had made sure there were no Japs around. I cooked on charcoal, which I made about once a week. I would cache what I could not carry. After awhile I had food, weapons and charcoal hidden in many places. You make charcoal by making a pile of wood and covering it with dirt, once lit. I had a saw to cut the wood with; chopping makes too much noise. Another need for charcoal was to boil water to make it safe. Even in the wild, the water is not always good. I had to boil more than a quart a day. I cooked a lot using Jap helmets; they also were good for making salt. I could catch fish and make salt from seawater."

I could see that the beer had loosened Tom's tongue, and he talked far more than I had hoped for. So I just sat back and tried to remember all I could.

"Joseph came to see me one day and he had with him an English captain who had escaped from the camp. The captain wanted to thank me for helping him escape. I said I didn't remember helping him. He was English; his name was Summersfield.

"Summersfield told me, 'I was on a work detail, cutting wood for the Japs about a week ago. You shot three of the six guards. I had a small cut, and while you were shooting, I saw my chance. I put a bit of blood in the middle of my forehead and fell to the side of the trail, rolled away and played dead. The Japs took one look and must have believed you had shot me. Also, they were in a hurry to get out of there. It took me awhile to find a guerrilla camp and get Joseph to bring me here. I am hoping you might help me get out of here—I mean back to our side, off this island. I'm a spitfire pilot.'

"I'll think on it," I said, "but hell, if there was a safe way off, don't you think I'd be gone by now? What the hell is a spitfire pilot doing here?"

"I was in Canada training and recruiting badly needed pilots, when I was sent home on a ship. We were torpedoed, and the ship that picked us up dropped us off at Bankok. I made it to Manila, trying to get a plane to India.

"Can you tell me any good news about the camp?" I made us some of my own kind of tea and waited till he found a soft place to sit.

"You want good news from that hellhole? There is a story going around that somehow the U.S. bombed Tokyo. No one believes it, but we hope it's true. Okay, we did finally get some of the Red Cross boxes that the Japs have been keeping. It happened like this: There was a soldier with a wooden leg, and one day, the second-in-command Jap was showing some visiting Jap officers around. He felt the guy with the wooden leg did not bow low enough or fast enough. That Jap thought he was funny; he had seen an old Tarzan movie and would go up to anyone with a lot of hair on his chest, pull the hair and say, 'You Tarzan, me Jane, and laugh. Well anyway, he tried to be funny and shot the guy in the leg for not bowing right. He meant to shoot him in the wooden leg as a joke, but shot the poor guy in his good leg. That Jap had his back to the guy rolling in pain on the ground as he told the other Japs. 'It's OK; it's a wooden leg.'Later, he must have felt bad, as he let them give out some of the Red Cross boxes they were keeping in the food storage shed. But they might have just been making room for bags of rice. The Japs had opened all the boxes and taken all the medicine and any pills.

"That is as close to good news as I can give. Men are dying of malnutrition, about fifty a day. All the prisoners are in groups of ten. If a man escapes, they shoot or behead the rest of his group. With me, it was different because they did not think it was an escape.

"By any chance, do you have some food? I don't remember what meat tastes like. Hell, I could eat a horse.

"Yes, give me some time and I can come up with something.

"You said, 'Eat a horse.' I did eat horsemeat a few times. It was a sad day for General Wainwright when he had to butcher the last cavalry mounts in May. But one time when I was in the Army we ate a horse, and that was something. We were on maneuvers in the Ozark Mountains, out of Camp Leonardwood. The mess sergeant and his crew must have had their minds back in the Civil War, judging by what they wanted to feed us. Salt pork, hard bread, beans and more beans. Morale was low. I said if they would let me take a horse and go into the hills for a day or two, I could get an elk. They believed me. There were no elk. I shot and dressed out an old horse and said it was elk meat. All were happy to have fresh meat, and one old-timer cavalry sergeant said he had been so hungry for meat he could have ate a horse. I said, 'You just did.' And he threw up all over himself. I got hell for it, but no big deal.

"I have some dried carabao meat—that's water buffalo—in a cache nearby. You should have been there when I got it. The natives asked me to shoot a wild, mean carabao that was tearing up their rice planting. All I had was the .22. I was trying to shoot him in the ear, when he charged me. *How am I going to stop a ton of charging beef with a .22?* I thought. Then I remembered the old-time elephant hunters with their black-powder guns They made the first shots in the knee. I did the same. It took over six hits to break its knee. Then when it fell, I shot it in the head. But we could not lift it and had to skin and cut the meat right there in the rice. I was worried a Jap plane would spot us.

132

"I can feed you and let you rest near here for a day or two. Your best bet is to go to see a coast watcher I know and let him use his radio to call Army headquarters in Australia about getting you on a supply sub that meets one of the guerrilla groups to the south. But you're too weak to make that trip now. It will take about thirty or forty days walking. If I can get help from the Huks—maybe a boat— that would cut the trip to two or three weeks. I won't know for several days.

"Joseph, come back in two days and take him to live with a tribe of natives to get him built-up for the trip.

"The Huks have an outpost they sometimes use only a day's walk from here. Joseph and I will take them a load of Jap rifles to trade.

"I pulled back some brush and exposed a pile of ten Jap Arisaka rifles, ammunition belts, a pack of shoes, plus some other gear. I told Joseph, 'Glad you came. I need your help to carry these. About half will do for now,' with a hint that I have more.

"Getting away turned out to be more difficult than I thought. The coast watcher had been given up to the damn Japs by one of the natives for the reward. All I could do was get Summersfield to a good guerrilla camp. They pleaded with me for help in finding quinine. I knew there was a black market in Manila. I also wanted to check on the Jap POW camp at Los Banos that was south of the city. That was the camp for the Army nurses and officers. Because of my dark skin, I took a chance and hid my .22 Browning, dressed as a Filipino native and made my way there in about two weeks.

"Because of my Indian background, it was not easy for me to take anything off the dead, but this was war. Over time, I had relieved a lot of dead Japs of their cash, rings and other things to trade. Since they had mined gold on Luzon before the war, I melted down and made what gold I had into what would pass for small nuggets. The only weapon I carried was a small knife, and I came close to using it when a damn Jap private slapped me in the face because I looked him in the eye.

"My trip did not start off very good. It took awhile to learn where to fine the black-market dealers without getting caught. I ended up killing two damn Japs in a hotel toilet. I was to meet a man in the hall outside the men's room at a cheap hotel. Two damn Japs headed my way; someone had pointed me out. I ducked in the men's room and looked for a weapon. When they came in, I hit the first in the face with the heavy, porcelain, toilet tank lid. It crushed his face and drove him back on the second Jap. I rushed and knocked them both down. The second one, who was now on his back under the first, could do nothing about the smashing blow from the lid to his head. No shots were fired, but there was a lot of noise. I left by the back door and made it to a boat to hide till dark.

"I was very shook up. It's one thing to shoot a man from a distance, but to kill in coldblood is something else. To this day, I can close my eyes and see the fear and shock in the eyes of that last damn Jap just before I drove the toilet lid like a pile driver in his forehead.

"I finally was able to trade gold for some Jap quinine, but did not get much.

"Since it was not too far to the POW camp at Los Banos, I went there to see what I could learn from the Filipinos about how the nurses were being treated. That was the camp they were in, I was told. It was doubtful I could rescue any, but I had to see the camp. It was only a little better than the other camps, a deliberate effort to treat the American POW's with the most intolerable living conditions—things like restrictions on water, even while there was plenty; the daily allowance was far below what was needed to stay alive. It took courage for those gals to endure the sadistic guards. There was nothing I could do, so I went back north, vowing to even things by making the damn Japs pay."

Stone Bear, or should I say Tom, stopped talking and looked at me. "There was a special feeling for the Army nurses by the GI's you know," he said.

"Tell me more about the nurses," I said.

"I can tell you a funny story. Well, it's also sad

and also as stupid as the Army can be" he said.

"There was a short nurse. Her name was Barbara and she was a Japanese-American from Hawaii. Before December 7th, she was very popular. The guys would all ask for her and she was well liked by the other nurses. Then came Pearl, and suddenly all her friends left her. They acted like she was the one who dropped the bombs.

"I ate a lot of the officers' and nurses' mess hall. That had to do with the way I gave the cooks wild game and fish. One day, she was all alone at a table, and I joined her. We talked a bit. We were the only ones at our table and two nurses came in. One, a tall blond from California, walked past our table and said, 'I'd rather stand than eat with a Jap or stinking Indian!' That hurt the girl from Hawaii.

"That night, just after dark but before lights-out, I went into the nurses' tent and put five or six large, live grasshoppers between the sheets of that blond nurse's bed. Then I told some of the guys. We waited—there was a scream that would peel bark off an oak tree. The blond came running out of her tent while tearing at her flimsy nightgown. She was half-naked and saw the guys whooping and catcalling. She went back in the tent, remembered the bugs, and came out dragging a blanket that she wrapped up in. A few days later, the Japanese nurse from Hawaii was picked up by MPs in a jeep, put on a bus and sent to a camp in California. She saw me and blew me a kiss. I think hers was one of the last planes to leave."

Tom, again, got that faraway look and I was sure he was back in the Phillipines.

"The damn Japs would go out on a ten-day patrol, so if I shot any before they were out too long, I could get food from their packs. Mostly, it was rice and some cans of fish. They had a reward out on me, and I could recognize the Jap name they gave me. I would be a lot closer than they believed. When the damn Japs I shot were found, that cry of 'Shadow Demon' would echo. I know the cutting off of balls had an effect.

"Would you believe it? I may be the only Marine to have stopped a Banzai charge single-handledly, and with a .22. Both the Japs and I were surprised when I climbed a ridge and there were a hundred or more heading toward me. I did not shoot at first, but ran back a few yards and took cover behind a bush till I could decide which way to go. I could hear my name and the officers telling them to charge and get the devil. Next thing I know, there are ten or more yelling Banzai running at me. I started shooting at heads, then switched and shot three or four in the balls. At that, they either stopped and hit the dirt or ran back to safety at the other side of the ridge. A few, no more than three were kneeling and trying to get a shot at me but still did not know exactly where I was.

"After I shot them, I ran like hell. After a few

yards, I hit a trail, so I planted a couple of grenades for their feet to hit. You take a frag grenade and jam it in the dirt, lever-side down, and pull the pin. Then put a stick or leaves on top. It goes off about six seconds after stepped-on or kicked. That slows down anyone chassing you. I ran for the first half-mile, then I switched to walking and leaving no tracks, but only after setting up a false trail.

"Did I tell you about leaving no tracks? Remember that I cut off Japs' pant legs. You slip that tube of cloth over your boot and tie the top. Then stuff it with grass, leaves, or whatever, and tie off the front. It pads the edges of your boots and spreads out your footprint. With that and careful placement, you can be trailed by only the best of trackers. The damn Japs never learned that trick.

"There was another use for the extra pant legs. I could slip them over my pants and stuff in between with grass or palm leaves. The one-inch layer gave me protection from snakebites. I traveled a lot during the dark, and snakes move at night; some are poisonous.

"It was then becoming too hot for me. I spent some time hiding with the pygmy and Moro tribes. They were pleased and found it hard to believe it when I made them some flint arrowheads. Captain Summersfield had found a guerrilla group to his liking, so I forgot about him. But for myself, the natives were suffering because of me. It was time I tried to get away.

"I was making my way toward the east coast and stopped to rest, when the birds told me something big was coming my way. I did a good job of hiding, and waited. Three very nervous Japs were walking point for a larger patrol. I was about to shoot one, when something didn't look right. I used my field glasses and saw that there were no bolts in the rifles of all three. They looked more like Filipinos than Japs. I let them pass. The last damn Jap in the patrol fell behind. I was thinking of shooting him, when he fell down. I got a close look; he was just a kid. I felt, *Hell, what's the point in killing him?*

"Then I heard three rifle shots and a scream; a scream I had heard before. The damn Japs had shot the three decoy Filipinos and were finishing one off with a bayonet. I shot that damn Jap, kid or not. I went looking for a coast watcher.

"The Australian coast watcher I found told me that there was a guerrilla group run by an American Army major not too far to the south. They were in contact with the Army headquarters and might be able to help. He also asked if by any chance I was a Navaho. He heard the Marines were looking for any GI that was a Navaho.

"We walked for many days, traveling mostly at dusk and dawn. About two days before reaching the place I was told to find, we heard the sound of a body running and crashing in the brush. As we got closer, I saw it was a damn Jap, and he was either

139

nuts or scared silly. He yelled a few times—in English, but so garbled I could not make out what he was saying. I aimed the .22 at his head and figured to shut him up, when he turned and in perfect English begged the Shadow Demon not to shoot him in the balls.

"Summersfield put his hand on my rifle and asked if maybe we should talk to him. I said OK, but you know, in guerrilla war you won't take prisoners. I yelled for the Jap to drop his rifle and not to move. He put his hands up, fell to his knees and begged for his life. Summersfield asked where he learned to speak so well. He said that he had been in America most of his life. His dad managed an import-export business in L.A. He was a student at UCLA when the war started. He even tried to get the FBI to send him to an internment camp. But since he was a Japanese national, he was sent back to Japan by way of Mexico.

"I asked if at UCLA he was engineering major, learning American science skills.

"No," he said he was a music major working on his master's in French horn. He said he would be willing to go with us and serve as an interpretor. We argued about taking him with us to the guerilla camp. He cut in to say he knew something useful for that camp. I put the .22 to his face and demanded what. He said the Japs had a spy in most camps and were planning to raid one camp. He knew what she looked like.

140

"So we took him and turned him over to the Army when we got there. I never found out what happened to him. I know the Filipinos wanted to hang him. One Filipino scout said, 'Hang him two times, and second time by the neck.'

"I took Captain Summersfield with me and went to see the major. I had known about him and his band for some time but stayed away for fear they might order me to join them. The major was not there. His staff told me to wait, since the major was off making arrangements for a sub drop-off. When I asked about the Navaho thing, all they could say was very little—something about training Navahos as radio operators. His men kept pestering me for details about shooting the damn Japs in the balls.

"Their leader, a Major Wilson, came back with an Army officer from MacArthur's command. He had been dropped off to coordinate the next drop and pick up any trained pilots, plus me. They had learned of my special war in Australia and wanted to see me. He hinted there would be a medal and a return to the States.

"When the sub came, they took six of us. The others told the sub's crew about what I had been doing, and the crrew treated me like I was special. The cook asked if there was anything I wanted to eat. I asked for and got a peanut butter and jelly on white bread. I asked if they had any coffee.

"Are you kidding?" He said. "This is the Navy.

We always have coffee."

"We were at sea about a week, and I could not get much sleep for answering questions about my private war with a .22, which I still had.

"Then one night when we were on the surface, a radio message came to the Army major. I was told to stop all talk about shooting Japs in the balls. When we got to the sub base at Pearl, I was told to stay in the captain's quarters while the Army major talked to the crew. I was informed tht MacArthur had ordered that there was to be a total censorship about shooting any Jap in the balls. His staff had a meeting and felt it might have bad repercussions if word got out to the world press. I was read some sections of the rules of war and was told to keep my mouth shut or I could be facing charges as a war criminal, plus court-martial for breaking Marine rules about mutilating the enemy dead. Then I learned that only the officers would get shore leave; they did not trust the crew to keep quiet when they went drinking. The crew was very pissed off at me, and it showed.

"I asked the medical corpsman if any crewmember that was sick would go to the base hospital. When he said yes, I made a tea from some of the pygmy herbs and put it in the coffeepot.

"While I waited, under guard, for the plane back to the States, I learned that because most all of the sub's crew were on shore in sickbay with the three-day shits, there was no point in keeping the rest on board. I had won that little fight, but I stayed away from the crew in case they didn't like the way I did it."

I asked Tom about how many Japs he killed. Did he count coups, since he was Indian?

"I never would keep track of something like that," he said. For an Indian to count coups, you don't have to even kill, just touch the enemy. Okay, most Indians would count coups on the enemy that they alone killed. I was too busy just staying alive to take time for that."

"Sorry I asked," I said. I was looking at my watch and it may have looked like I didn't see, but I'm sure I saw his finger write a number on the bar with the wet from the beer. It was 263. Then I remembered that he had started with ten boxes of fifty .22 shells. Allowing for shooting food, that number made sense.

Tom stopped speaking, got up, and went to the men's room, mumbling about recycling beer. When he came back, he suddenly grabbed me by the front of my belt, pulled me off the barstool, and whipped out a long knife. I dared not move. Then he let me loose and said, "Now you can write about war. You know about fear."

A tall cop came to the door and called him. I heard him say, "What did you do, Dad?"

"That's his son, said the bartender. "You were lucky. That Indian is a real head case. When he is done at the VA hospital, his son meets him here."

I left, borrowing two issues of the VFW magazine to keep my car seat dry.

THE END

THE LUCKY BOTTLE OF GIN

I was flying a C-47 transport as a member of the 10th U.S. Army Air Force stationed in India. We hauled supplies to the U.S. and British forces that were aiding the Chinese in their fight to keep the Japs out of Burma. We flew the 'Hump' many times with as heavy a load as possible. After one flight that had too many close calls, it dawned on me that I was maybe the only pilot that did not have some kind of good luck charm. I've never been superstitious and only gave the matter any thought till after that flight and the way my co-pilot kissed a picture and lucky coin his girl gave him. We were just too busy for me to take much time trying to find what would be my good luck charm.

"Your plane is loaded, Sir," said the ground crew chief.

"Already?" I questioned. I had just got to the hanger and poured a cup of coffee.

"It's not a full load, but the Brit's are in a hurry for you to take one of their officers to Mangoon."

"At the plane, I found my co-pilot, a British Captain and his Gurkha aid, complete with one of those funny knifes they carry. Tied to the cargo bay hooks were a few boxes of medical supplies, and not tied down were two cases of Gordon Gin packed in wood, but open on top. Over my objections, the Brit would not let our crew touch the gin. They would hold onto the boxes with straps that they had been given for that purpose.

"Three hours into our flight, as we were weaving through the mountain passes, the plane hit a down draft that caused us to drop like a rock for several hundred feet. Right then, as we came out of thick clouds, we were looking straight ahead at the top of some tree! Together, the co-pilot and I pulled back on the sticks till we were in an almost straight-up climb. The treetops brushed our plane, but we made it back where it was safe to level off. I had heard a crash from the cargo bay, and went back for a look. There was broken glass and gin all over the plane. With difficulty I could make out two bodies tangled up with the medical supplies in a ball at the back of the plane. At first, it looked like they were dead, but then I saw that they were breathing. Jammed next to the side door was an empty gin case, only when I went to move it, I found one bottle flat on the bottom still in as virgin state as when first sold. I picked it up and looked for a good place to hide it. Our own first-aid pouch that was fixed to the wall was just the right size. The gin bottle fit in after I took out most of the emergency supplies and put them in my pockets. I had to use some of them to deal with the many small cuts on the bare legs of my two very upset passengers. "There's to be bloody hell over this flight!" Threatened the English Captain. There was a major ass-chewing for me and my co-pilot, but nothing more after we assured our CO that I had warned the limey to tie down his precious cargo of gin. I was all set to share that Gin with my buddies till it was said 'that sure is a lucky bottle of Gin!'

"I refused to share the gin, and declared the bottle as my own lucky charm. The ground crew helped me make a safe holder for the bottle out of the sheets of cork used to make gaskets for our motors. That bottle protected me through many more flights, even a few over Japan when I was transferred to a B-17.

"I carried the gin on a B-25 equipped for ground strafing over Korea. Many times my plane was hit, but never shot down while I had my lucky bottle of Gin. After Korea, I decided to stay in and by 1956, I was flying an F-89 Jet. There again, it saved me.

"One of my fellow pilots was not so lucky over Maine when a training exercise got fouled up. EADC, Eastern Air Defense Command was about to schedule an emergency training mission for the whole east coast. They were waiting for every squadron that had to rotate it's armed planes to have completed the rotation before sounding the 'Alert'.

"At that time every squadron that had a defense commitment would have a number of planes, say maybe six or so fully armed and ready with crews to take off for a set number of days. At our base, there was a breakdown in the carts used to carry the heavy air-to-air missiles. The armament crew, rather than have fewer than the right number of planes armed, decided to first move two armed planes out of the alert pods, and onto the flight line. A crew member was stationed with each of these 'HOT' planes to prevent their use till the missiles could be downloaded. The first thing to go wrong was when the command center called and was told that there were now six new planes armed and in the alert pods. The plane numbers were given, as well as the numbers of the planes now off alert status and usable. The airman that made that report did not know that as soon as this was reported to eastern headquarters, a recall type of alert exercise would be sounded. All personnel reported for duty and as many planes would be sent up as possible. Only those in the alert pods would not take part. On the flight line near the alert pods, the first of the two armed 'Hot' planes was downloaded of it's real missiles and re-armed with the dummy missiles used to training in alerts just like this one. Because of the alert, the head of the ground crew replaced the guard on the one still-armed plane with a new airman; one that would not be as useful as the man that had been there. The new man was carefully informed that he was to stay with that plane Number 8151 because it was 'HOT'. No one had bothered to tell him what the term 'HOT stood for. It was learned later that he had raced Hotrod cars and was of the impression that 'HOT' only meant that it was a fast plane.

"I had been nearby when the alert alarm went off, and was one of the first to get the number of an approved plane, and with a friend, we both took off and flew a type of sweeping mission to search out any enemy planes. In a new padded pocket on the side of my leg was my lucky bottle of Gin. We had standing orders to make a mock attack, using our dummy missiles on only military planes we saw. Only civilian planes were off limits. It would not be a good idea to jam the radar or scare an airliner full of vacationing people.

"One of our pilots was a great distance from the base, and got here to find no planes left in the usual parts of the flightline. He checked with the operations-ready room chart and saw the number of a plane not checked off as in use, or out of commission or on armed alert status. He sucked oxygen to clear his head of the nights' beer and headed for the flightline. He found plane 8151 and asked the young airman standing next to it to help him move a starting generator from nearby. The pilot wondered why that plane was still there. He asked the airman if there was a problem with it. 'No, Sir, she's a fast one, they say,' was what the Pilot told the investigating team. Maybe because it was winter and he had on heavy gloves, and maybe his head was not too clear, that his drinking was not measured as a danger. Maybe he was just trying too hard that he did not see the red tags on his missile arming switches and thinking he was only equipped with dummy missiles—the kind that would record his radar scope and instruments during his "attack" on another plane. He was just reaching the search area flying F-89 8151, when his radar found my plane and my wing man that was on my left. Near the end of our fuel range for a peacetime mission, we were returning to base. Of the two planes in his radar's view, 8151 picked the F-89 on his right. I was flying the one on his left. His voice recorder picked up his amazed cry, "MY GOD I'M HOT!" Just seconds before his missiles blew the plane next to me into a million pieces. My lucky Gin bottle had saved me again. In the accident investigation, the main blame fell on the guy that reported all the armed planes as being returned to safe status.

"Together with two fishing buddies, I became the proud owner of a cabin and fifty feet of land on the Current River in the Ozarks hills of Missouri. I was there checking on the work of three redneck local workers who were digging our cabin a new septic tank. Above the bar I mounted a propeller from a small plane and I was ready to mount a special oak shelve above it for my lucky bottle of Gin. I left the gin and shelf on the bar and went to get a ladder.

"Yes, have a beer!" I replied to one of the redneck workers as I went to get the ladder from the shed. It took awhile to dig the stepladder from under the pile of old boards left from making our boat dock. The redneck crew thanked me as they went back to work. On the bar I found three empty beer cans and flat on its side, my lucky Gin bottle, empty! Its luck had run out. So help me, as I stormed out to have a few words with the rednecks the step broke. I fell and broke my ankle. Waiting for the doctor, all I could think of was how I was going to miss that bottle of gin. I recalled a line of wisdom from an old Air Force bartender who said, "Funny thing, the poor drink straight gin while the rich drink very dry martinis."

THE END

THE CARD ROOM

Sergeant Berry Locke waved at his fellow non-commissioned officers as he pointed to the squadron bulletin board.

"What's it about?" asked Sergeant Lewis Grant.

"It says, By order of the Provost Marshal, enlisted men may not keep any firearms in their cars. Not in closed gun cases or in the trunk. ALL private guns must be stored in the armory or in a secure locker in supply. A sign-out sheet will be used at all times.

"Nuts! Small game season starts next week. The armory is seldom open, and supply only from eight to four. Let's go see the first sergeant. I know he keeps both a shot gun and a deer rifle in the trunk of his old Ford," said Sergeant Lee Monroe. Sergeant Al Kent joined them as they rushed to catch the first sergeant before he left for the chow hall.

Berry, Lewis, Lee and Al were instructors in either the radar or radio training schools at this base in Colorado. All were single and so lived in one of the newer brick barracks. Their main off duty sport was hunting and shooting. First for small game, then deer and other big game. In between hunting seasons, they shot at targets or clay pigeons.

The first sergeant was not helpful. "Sorry, men, but I already tried. I saw that the hours of supply were not good for morning hunting. I asked about your getting the guns from supply and keeping them closed in car trunks or wall lockers just overnight. No deal. The provost marshal is a New York City boy, and he hates guns. You might try one of your married buddies that lives off base."

None of the married men wanted to ask their wives about a bunch of guys waking them at four in the morning every Saturday during hunting season.

During lunch, many ideas were considered. Berry had one that could be promising. They would go see Airman First Class Duncon in the orderly room.

"Duncon, old buddy, I seem to remember you wanted us to take you hunting last year. I think it's time you join our group. There is only a small favor we would need. That end room, the only single room in barracks 904, the sergeant that is in it is shipping out soon. You make the room assignments. If you could keep that room open, we could use the locker there to hide our hunting guns. That room was empty for a while back, and we used it as a card room. What you say? You want us to take you hunting?"

"No way. I could get in trouble. And you're too late. I was just told to house an old timer sergeant from motor pool there. He's getting a medical discharge in six weeks and had to be moved back on base for his treatment.

"What kind of treatment? Can't you put him in some other barracks? Come on, think of a way to keep that room free for us. We would keep your guns there too," teased Berry.

"No one told me what his medical problem is. I know that no one wanted him. As for keeping a room empty, they sometimes check on my housing lists. I would have to list a made-up name. There would be hell to pay if I got caught. Sorry."

The next afternoon, they returned from work to find that Sergeant Kinwick had moved into the card room. He had been in the Air Force for twenty-eight years. His plan to reach thirty was cut short because of his drinking problem. He was an alcoholic. They were giving him a medical discharge and counseling every day till the discharge processing paperwork was complete.

Kinwick stumbled in at 2 a.m. waking them with his cursing and puking in the hallway and latrine. He outranked them and would try to use his rank to make others clean up when he puked in the hall. One night when they found him sleeping with his door open, and a bright bare light bulb left on, Lee turned off the light and closed his door. The smell from his room was getting to them and they were considering how they could get him to move. The next morning, he came screaming and banging on their doors. The four shared two rooms next to Kinwick's.

"Who in the hell. What mother turned off my light? Don't ever do that! They almost got me!" After more cursing and warnings, he left for his daily visits to the base hospital.

With the start of small game hunting season, the four stored their deer rifles at the supply office. The shotguns used for bird hunting were disassembled and the parts hidden. Most were tied to coat hangers and hung inside of dress uniforms covered with plastic.

"It won't make him move, and we will end up cleaning up the mess if the dog shits in our barracks," said Al.

"It's worth doing just to get back at him," said Lee as he led the dog away from the chow hall with a hot dog. They had found the mangy mutt knocking over garbage cans. It was a big black dirty beast that they put in Kinwick's room while he was out drinking.

They left their room doors ajar and listened for Kinwick's reaction to the dog, till they all fell asleep. At 5 a.m., there was a crash as Kinwick knocked his door half off its hinges escaping from his room. He was swinging a baseball bat and ran about outside swinging the bat at some imaginary beast till they came and got him with a white straight jacket. His gear was moved to storage the next day and it was explained that Kinwick would stay in the hospital till discharged. Berry learned from a nurse that the dog had been under Kinwick's bed and breathed in his face when he rolled over. He was sure it was the breath of the devil. Now the card room was empty.

Al was skeptical. "Berry, you really think if we take Duncon hunting and he gets a big buck that will get him to hold the card room for our guns?"

"It won't hurt to try," said Berry.

"That's right, Duncon old buddy, we want you to go deer hunting with us this Saturday. I'll pick you up at 04:30, dress warm. Since you're new to where we are hunting, you will be posted and may very likely get a shot at a deer which we'll drive past your stand."

Lee was a good half mile from the stands of Duncon and Berry, who was nearby in case Duncon missed. He had heard a lone shot, then he met the farmer driving a tractor. The farmer recognized Lee as one of the men that had asked his permission several days before. He stopped to talk. "I had to shoot a sick cow. It's back in the field above the creek. Don't want you boys to think you did it." Then he drove on. Lee was quick to see the possibilities. He approached Berry and whispered a plan.

Lee left and walked so that Duncon could see him. Berry called to Duncon. "Come with me. Lee knows where there is a buck that is bedded down. He will get on the west side of it and put Al on the east. I'll take you to it from the south, that way you should get a safe shot when we jump him."

Duncon carried his Winchester at a ready position. Berry could see the sweat building on Duncon's forehead.

"There he is. See his horns sticking up in the brush?"

"I don't see any deer."

"Look closer to the ground. There to the right of the tree with the double trunk, see the horns behind the branches?" exclaimed Berry as he pointed. "Look, he's getting up. SHOOT!"

At Berry's urging, he shot.

"Good shot. Didn't you hear him fall?"

"I still don't see any deer."

They walked towards the woods on the edge of the open field of tall grass till Berry stopped and pointed to one side.

"Good God, Duncon, look! You shot a cow! I knew we should have had you do some targets."

Duncon was almost in shock. "What'll we do?

157

How much does a cow cost?"

Berry called to Lee and Al. "Take Duncon back to the car. I'll go find the farmer and see what I can work out."

Once they left, he sat and drank a cup of coffee from his back pack.

"He was mad as all get out," Berry lied. "Only because he can salvage the meat did he agree to let you off for four hundred dollars. I paid him with a loose check I keep in my wallet. Consider it a loan."

"I can't come up with that much. I only get fifty-two and my car payments is forty-three."

Berry looked at Lee, Al and Lewis. "There is a way, since we took you hunting and our pay is bigger than yours. We cover the cost of the cow you shot and you get us that card room."

"How can I do that?"

"Work on it, or come up with four hundred, that's the deal. Just list the name of some guy that shipped out that was not well known, a common name. Make it look like the room is occupied."

Duncon came through. The name Sergeant Bill Rodgers was posted on the card room door. Extra uniforms were hung there. A foot locker was added, as well as shined boots under the cot. A combination lock on the steel locker made a safe place for their guns. The room was kept shipshape and Sergeant

Bill Rodgers' name was added to lists on the barracks bulleting board as a member of the bowling and softball teams.

Two other NCOs that lived down the hall were allowed to add their guns to keep them from talking.

Lewis almost screwed it up one night in the NCO Club when after many pitchers of beer, he said, "If we are ever attacked, forget the armory, I'm heading for the card room. I can get a gun there without red tape." He was quickly told to shut his trap.

An inspection of rooms was held by the new second lieutenant. He announced at roll call that the winner was Sergeant Bill Rodgers. He was called to step forward to receive a certificate of recognition.

"He's on sick call," said Berry.

"Then send him to the first sergeant when he gets back. I'll be away for a week."

Before the guys could come up with a man from another squadron to fake being Bill Rodgers, the first sergeant called Berry and Lee to his office. He shut his door and told them to stand at ease.

"Men, I'm trading my old Ford in on a new VW. It has a trunk way too small for my guns. That means, I'll need the combination to your gun locker in the card room. I'll say that Sergeant Rodgers has been transferred and have Duncon make up a new name for that room. Dismissed."

THE MARSHMALLOW SQUAD

The sergeant barked, "You five get your rifles and bayonets, NOW!"

Dunmore was slow to get up from his seat around the campfire. He grinned and sat back down when the sergeant waved him to sit and yelled for Big Mike to take his place. The men quickly returned and as prompted, fixed bayonets on their MI rifles.

WWII fighting men about to go into action? Not hardly. Not hardly by a long shot. That summer morning the men of Second Platoon, C for Charlie Company, 105th Mechanized Infantry Battalion of the Pennsylvania National Guard fell out of their warm barracks with full field packs ready for three days of bivouac at Camp Drum in upstate New York.

"Okay, men, drop your gear, spread and open for inspection," yelled Sergeant Counts. He put up with the grumbling for a very short time. He was about to start chewing ass when a jeep pulled up and the driver delivered a message.

"At ease. Looks like the trucks will be an hour late. Stand by your gear, yes, smoke if you got 'em."

"Hey, sergeant, I was here last year. We could

walk to the bivouac area in half an hour. Why wait for the trucks?" said a middle school teacher.

"Because this is a mechanized unit. The truck drivers also need practice. And never, but never turn down a ride. We ever get to see real action, you'll learn that." He kicked a rolled up blanket and out fell a pint of whiskey.

"What do I have here?" he waved to some that were drifting away. "Pay attention. This is why I'm checking your gear." He pointed to the private that had suggested they walk. "You, Wilson, tell these guys about last year's marshmallow disaster."

Wilson sat on a five gallon water can and began. Sergeant Snyder was trying to make a point about teamwork around a campfire last year. He had five guys hold MIs with bayonets and then to their surprise, he put a marshmallow on the tip of each and told them to roast the marshmallow but not to eat until told. Then he said, "Feed each other without using your hands." They paired off, but with five guys, one man was left out. Then he gave the four new marshmallows and after they were roasted, had the men form a circle and feed the guy next to him, going around so they could see all got fed. He made them do it faster, and did not see one guy fill a canteen cup with ice, coke and rum for a half pint from his pack. The kid standing next to him was hit right in his eye by a burning marshmallow that flew off a bayonet as his buddy tried to shake off the flames. The guy with the rum and coke immediately dumped his canteen cup in the face putting out the flames. The screaming and swearing brought a lieutenant who sent for a nurse. The nurse came and saw that the guy's eye was plastered over with stiff marshmallow. She made him keep his hands off the glob of marshmallow.

"The best I can do is cover it with a clean wet cloth and send him to the base hospital," she said. "The quick action of your friend dumping the cold drink might have saved your eye. A doctor will know what to do. What's your name?" she said, as she tried to keep him calm.

"Private Dean Spears. I'm from Boyds Mills. Do you think I'll lose my sight? At least it's not my shooting eye."

When the bandages in the first aid kit proved too small, she opened her purse. She covered his eye with a white pad tying it around his head like a pirates eye patch. He could not see what she was putting on him. His buddies' smirks were a clue he missed.

At the hospital, they found he had blinked in time and only his eye lid was blistered and his eyebrow hair was burned off.

"Quick action, and good innovative first aid saved your eye, young man," said the doctor with a grin and wink at the nurse.

"He was lucky a cold drink was there," said the

nurse.

A staff officer there to check on the accident smelled the rum and said he would have to report that the accident was surely the result of drinking. It was explained to him how the private got covered with rum, so he said he would not report the drinking. When he did type his accident report, he could not bring himself to write the accident was the result of a marshmallow roast. He reported the eye was hit by the point of a bayonet. Getting hit by a bayonet resulted in the paper work for a Purple Heart award for Private Spears. By the time that paper got to the captain, he knew all about the marshmallow roast and killed the award.

The lucky private never learned that his picture was on the bulletin board at the emergency room wearing a Kotex sanitary pad.

PAIR-OF-DICE ISLAND

It may have been the noise of pounding surf or the smell of land that woke him from his stupor. Ten days on the tiny raft, four without water, had moved the lad past the halfway point to death's doorstep. It was 1944 and Lieutenant David Wood splashed water over his face and questioned his senses. *Did I die? Is that to be my heaven?* He lifted his head for a better view over the peaks of waves that were driving him towards the island and the three white gorgeous young women standing on the sand, waving at him as they jumped up and down. The jumping resulted in an oscillating motion of their breasts. He stretched out extending both arms to paddle with. Only by his youth did he find the energy to make his body try. The raft's tiny wood paddle was long lost to sharks that must have decided the strange yellow raft would have no more food value than the paddle. The waves crested higher and higher as they reached the beach, at last dumping him a good thirty feet from safety. Each of his efforts to stand failed as the force of the water tore him forward and then back. He tried to get air just as his head went under again. In panic, he crawled on the sea floor. This last disappearance was too much for Nurse Kimberly Moyer. She swam out and pulled him in till the water was mere inches. There, the other girls helped drag the gagging lad up the beach to dry sand.

His first words were, "What are you doing here?" But with all speaking at the same time, there was no answer. It was a noisy chorus of questions.

"What's your name?" "Are you hungry?" "Where did you come from?" "Are Japs coming here?"

He held up a hand, and through cracked lips asked, "Do you have water?"

While falling all over themselves, the girls helped him stand and two led him to the shade of a patch of parachute while the third carried him a drink in half of a coconut shell.

He found himself too weak to stand and sat bracing his back on one of the palm trees.

"I take it you're stranded here. Do you know where we are?"

Their nods told him they did not.

"We must be on one of the outer Solomons. Have you been here long? How did you get here?"

"First off, I'm Lieutenant Monica Hamilton. This is Lieutenant Candice Young, and the tall one if Lieutenant Kimberly Moyer. Yes, all Navy nurses. We were on a flight from Rabaci to Australia when Jap fighters attacked our Red Cross plane. The pilot was hit and the gas tanks. He found this island and he had us parachute near the beach, then he was to ditch in the shallows, but his plane flipped and went down. We never saw him. A high wind moved the plane out to sea from where we could see the tail sticking up. There's lots of fruit here, but not much else. Kim had a pair of dice in her pocket so we named this Pair-O-Dice Island. What about you? I'm a mean judge of young GIs and you don't look old enough to be in the service, much less as a pilot. How old are you? Say you aren't wearing dog tags. Where are they?"

"I lost them to a shark. I was using them to attract fish. Here, look at my I.D. card." He flashed a GI I.D. card, then put it back into his wallet.

"I didn't get to see your birth date. How old are you?"

Dave took a deep breath. "You say you're nurses? I've had no food for a week. We can talk later. Looks like we'll have lots of time."

The girls agreed and gave him a mango.

"Are you getting food from the sea?"

"We tried to catch fish with a spear, but no luck, and no knife or fire if we did."

"Let me rest a bit and I'll treat you to a New England clam bake." He rolled over and hid his eyes with a well tanned arm and went to sleep.

He woke to find the girls gathering firewood

and Kim struggling to light a pile of it with his Zippo lighter.

"Here, let me show you how, and I'll take charge of my lighter if you please. You're wasting what fuel it has left, 'cause it looks like you need to learn how to make a fire."

"First, we dig clams. I'll need rocks, lots of driftwood, large leaves and we dig a ditch."

He started the nurse that reminded him he could call her Candy to digging a ditch as deep as her forearm and three feet long. He took Monica and Kim to the edge of the water.

"The tide is going out. See these little air holes? Watch this."

He furiously dug, and soon pulled out a clam. When there were a few more, he took off his shirt and began to pile the clams on it. The nurses got better with practice and as soon as there was a good pile started, he left them and showed Candy how to use grass to start a fire, then add bigger and bigger pieces of wood. She led him to a stream where they picked up rocks. He placed the rocks on the fire that was now filling the ditch.

"More wood and rocks." He used his pocket knife to cut large green leaves that he took to the water's edge and wet down.

"Now we wait." Once the fire was just red coals

and water hissed on the rocks, he put in the ditch a layer of wet leaves and then the clams, then more wet leaves, and to their surprise, covered them with sand till the ditch was gone, and the only way you could tell where it had been was the steam that drifted up from the sand.

"How long?"

"About forty-five minutes to an hour. Is there a watch? I lost mine."

"No, can you make a sun dial?"

He then sat down and began to recite a poem that began with a drunk walking into a bar.

"What's this dinner theater?" asked Kim.

"Please, don't stop me again. See this stick I put here? It takes me fifteen minutes to do The Face on the Barroom Floor. I'll mark how long the shadow is, then times three, plus a little extra for the changing angle of the sun.

The nurses sat while he said the whole poem. He made his marks to judge time, and asked what they used for drinking. They showed him bowls made from coconuts. He went to the life raft and untied his GI canteen and removed its cup. "We can cook fish soup in this."

"While we wait for the clams, I never got an answer about how you got here. Or your age," asked

Candy.

"Okay, I'm not as old as I should be, for my duties that is. I got my first pilot's license when I was fourteen. My grandfather has a flying service. He does crop-dusting and charter flights all over the Midwest. We live in central Illinois, New Effingham. I started going with him about age nine. I was doing navigating by ten. I started to fly solo at twelve. He was a WWI Ace, and a close friend, a hunting buddy of Senator Paul Simson. I joined the Army Air Corps at seventeen. Thanks to a word from the senator, I got a chance to go to flight school even with the rules calling for age eighteen. It was in the last week of training when I f... screwed up and got kicked out."

"What happened?"

"I had a bunk mate that drove the general, the base commander's car. A Buick convertible. I saw him and did not see that the general's wife was in the back seat. I buzzed them so close my prop hit the car's radio antenna. The general's wife dropped a load in her white party dress. The general had me kicked out of flight school, and he tried to send me to the infantry.

"My C.O. transferred me to navigator's school. In two weeks I was helping teach the new students and those that had problems. The general found out where I was and was cutting new orders for me when the head of the navigator's school rushed the paperwork and graduated me. They shipped me to Seattle. I got there as they needed to fly some maps out here. We were heading back to Australia when the Jap zeros caught our C-46. The zeros must have been short on fuel, 'cause they made one pass, both of them fired on the cabin. The pilot and co-pilot were killed, but not me. I flew into the clouds and circled till they were gone, and then learned a fuel tank had taken a hit. I ditched and drifted here. Let's eat."

The nurses all pitched in removing the sand, palm leaves and then the steamed clams.

The next day, Dave cut up a parachute and made four hammocks, three for the nurses in one area and one for him nearby. Like a Boy Scout, he soon had them organized with duties for every day. There was gathering wood for cooking and the setting up of four signal fires, one on each side of the island. Fish traps he had made had to be checked and a more detailed exploring of the island was started.

On the far side, they found two strong poles in the water.

"That was part of a boat dock," he pointed out. They moved straight inland from there where the growth of palms was thick. Pushing the undergrowth aside, he found lumps of coal.

"This might have been a refueling station for some shipping company years ago. Look for signs of a building."

"How about an old truck?" said Candy.

There in a gully, Dave found what was left of a truck body, no motor, but what might have been a dump. A few broken tools were found, and Dave was able to pull a side mirror off.

"We can use this for signaling."

"Here's a real treasure," called Kim as she dug up most of a shovel. My nails will welcome this."

Dave found several wine and beer bottles that he began to clean out with sand. Probing with a broken pipe, Candy found a pile of sheet metal roofing.

"That could make us a roof," said Kim.

"No, I might be able to make a boat with this and a frame of bamboo," said Dave.

"Why would we risk going to sea in a makeshift boat. Aren't we better off here?"

"The boat is in case Japs get here first. You don't want to know what would happen to you girls if Japs find us. All I have is one pistol and three shells. We would try and hide and use the boat to get away in the night. I'll figure out how to make it safe."

The next morning, cutting with a broken glass bottle, the nurses used the parachutes to make togas that they wore while washing their uniforms and under garments. Seeing the girls in these outfits was a strain for Dave. Kim was the first to mention a change.

"Have you noticed how Dave disappears two or three times a day. And when we find him, he is resting. He's not the working tiger he was at first. Could he be getting sick?"

"No, Kim. I'll make a guess. Here he is on an island with three females wearing next to nothing and we treat him like a kid brother. The boy is just horny. Don't you know about 'spanking-the-monkey?'"

"What's that."

"She's trying to tell us the boy is masturbating a lot."

"What's the solution, balling him?"

"Would it kill us if he got a little sex once in a while?" said Candy. "But since I'm the only one married, it's up to you two."

Candy went into the hut Dave had made for himself. She returned with his I.D. card. "Look at this. It's his birthday tomorrow. He will be eighteen!"

Kim took our her pair of dice and spread a cloth. "One roll each, high number breaks his virginity tonight."

"No, we should work up to it. Foreplay tonight and sex on his birthday, the first night when he's eighteen."

"Just like that? Let's plan this out a little," said Monica. "I say we be up front with him. Something like, 'Dave, we really appreciate your being here. For a birthday present we ALL will go for a swim after dinner, yes skinny dipping, and when it's dark, one of us will sleep with you. Just that what happens on this island stays on the island when we get rescued.'" She rolled the dice as did the other two. Candy saying, "What the hell, there's a war on," as she rolled the high number.

Dave came running past them. He grabbed a string and tied the truck mirror around his neck, and using his belt and bare feet, began to climb the largest palm tree.

"It's a ship, way out there. I think it's a carrier. I saw a Navy Hell Cat two days ago."

From the tree, he flashed with the mirror till the ship was out of sight.

"No reply, but that don't mean they did not see me."

The string broke and he dropped the mirror. Kim ran and picked it up. "It's not broke, thanks to the soft sand."

As she bent over to pick up the mirror, Dave

could see down the front of the toga she was wearing. He all but fell from the tree and started to leave, "I got to check on the boat."

"Hold on," said Candy as she took his arm. "I will go with you. We have something to talk over."

"Can't it wait? I'll be back soon."

"No, it can't."

Kim jumped up. "Dave, it's so hot. It's time we all went for a swim." She took hold of his arm and Candy grabbed the other. They set him on the sand at the water's edge. Monica broke the silence.

"Dave, here we are all alone on this island, you a boy, I mean a man, and the three of us. You have been so good for us, we need to repay you, and here's how."

Kim interrupted. "Also, as nurses, we have an obligation to see to your health."

"I'm fine," Dave said as he tried to get up.

"We have decided that we owe you a birthday present, but we have no place to shop," said Kim who broke out laughing.

Candy grabbed the confused lad and planted a hard kiss. "There is one thing we can give you as a gift and for your mental health," she said while giggling.

"We are all going swimming," cried Monica as she dropped her toga, grabbed his pants by the cuff and pulled.

They dragged him into the water. His face as red as the erection he sported.

"Tonight, you get the second part of your present. When one of us will sleep with you. It's for the good of our country. For the war effort! We need a healthy man on this island."

Dave stayed shy and in water up to his neck, as the girls let loose with a water fight and freely teased him about tonight, trying to make him guess who would slip into his bed.

A small power boat circled the island just out of range of small arms fire.

Scanning the beach with his field glasses the Lt. J.G. dropped them and pointed, "Holy Mother! Hard left rudder! Girls! Not natives, white women, three of them, full speed!"

He was dragged and almost choked by the strap as the Petty Officer and a Marine sergeant fought for his glasses. Their struggle blocked others from seeing ahead so they leaned over almost capsizing the boat.

A boat horn caught them by surprise. It was a Navy cutter, the service boat carried on ships. And there were sailors leaning all over the front as it headed into the breaking waves a hundred yards off the beach. All ran for cover and quickly dressed behind the parachute sides of their huts. Dave said to himself, "No! No! Not now!"

A squad of fully armed Marines were the first to land. Dave met them and explained there were no Japs. Just him and three stranded nurses.

At the ship the first officer asked for his dog tags, and then settled for his I.D. card.

"What's this, tomorrow, your birthday. This must sure be a lucky day for you."

"Not really."

He was starting to say they were a few days early when Candy pushed her way to him. She gave him a hug and big kiss and said, "Thanks for so much. Now remember our agreement, 'What happens on the island stays on the island."

Kim and Monica then each kissed him and said much the same. "We couldn't have made it without you, now what the nights were like will be our secret."

Monica punched his arm hard, and in a bedroom whisper, said, "Good luck, Stud." As the nurses were led away, a sailor stopped Dave, bowed low and saluted.

"Luckiest guy in the whole war," he exclaimed.

A PASS TO PARIS

"Hey! Look by the train, that's Sergeant Rossi. ROSSI, wait up! He can't hear me. Jeff, put your long legs to good use and catch him."

Corporal Jefferson ran and pushed his way through the crowd, grabbing Rossi as he was about to board.

"Jeff! How the hell are you? Where's Mutt?"

Private first class Matt Plummer and his buddy Corporal Jefferson Jordan were tagged Mutt and Jeff back in basic training; the names stuck. Matt was five foot four, had no neck and was built like a beer barrel. He grew up in Chicago and was a sharp man with cards, dice and, if needed, his fists. Jefferson, on the other hand, was six foot five, thin except for his broad shoulders and had a great charming smile. He hailed from the back hills of Southern Illinois. Caught making moonshine, the judge and he allowed that joining the Army was a better option than six months on a prison work farm.

Sergeant Rossi shook hands with both Matt and Jeff. "How the hell are you bums? What's this? You two as M.P.s! That proves the Army is FUBAR. Wish I'd met you guys before now. "I've got a pass for three days. Paris, here I come." He pulled on Matt's M.P. armband.

"I'll make it short, don't want you to miss your train. We were in the hospital, me with bits of Kraut steel in my back, and Jeff with a mild case of frostbite. His feet are too far from his heart. At the replacement center they said that with all the territory we had kicked the Germans from, the need for M.P.s was high. How come you get to go to Paris?"

"My squad captured a German colonel, his aide and their car. See you guys, here goes my train. Wait, just for old times sake."

He whispered in Jeff's ear, and jumped on the train, yelling, "You didn't hear that from me.

"What'd he say?"

Jeff cupped his hand, looked around and told Matt in a soft voice. "He was at H.Q. and learned the new script arrived. In a next day or so, the old script will be worthless. Well almost, like before there will be a cap on how much anyone can trade in for the new. That means we don't want to get caught with that big roll you won at poker from the Limeys."

During the war, the military issued their own type of money, called script. G.I.s were paid with it, as well as its use to local merchants for purchases. To hold down on black market dealings, the script would be recalled and a newer issue would be put out. No one was told when that was done. There would be both a time period and limits on dollar values on the old issue that could be turned over. After that the old script was worthless.

Mutt and Jeff made plans to take off the M.P. armbands that night and find card games where the script could be exchanged for cash. They were directing traffic as a rear hospital unit was loading up to move forward. Matt saw a Red Cross lady throwing some games into the trashcan.

"What's this?" he asked, as he opened a cardboard box.

"It's play money for dice and backgammon, but they stole the dice."

As soon as she was gone, Matt stuffed the paper play money in his shirt.

Off duty they went from bar to bar, telling the French that they had an early issue of the new script, the old would be worthless in about two days. For a good exchange rate, they could spare some of the new, since the French was treating them so well. The play bills soon became over several hundred in real script.

Directed to a back room they found a black market store. The Frenchman had U.S. leather fleece lined flight jackets just barely trimmed to look like civilian jackets. "I think this would be great to ship home, one for me and one for each of my brothers."

"Good idea, Matt. I'll take three myself."

After dickering over the price and showing an M.P. armband, they got a rock bottom price for the six jackets. Purchases paid for with the still good, but old script. Then Matt told the Frenchman he had been so good to them he would let him in on the fact that in a day or two, maybe even tomorrow, the script would change. He just happened to have three hundred of the new issue. He would trade it for two hundred in real U.S. dollars. The grateful man fell for it.

"Matt, if you had a conscious it sure would be bothering you after this deal."

"Where have you been? Just weeks ago when we liberated them, these frogs were handing us flowers and wine. Now they steal anything they can, overcharge us on anything we buy, and make disparaging remarks behind our backs. I'm beginning to feel they deserved what the Krauts did here."

The next morning, the two volunteered to be the first M.P.s moving into the next town where they would have to find and set up a new M.P. headquarters. In hours they were across the Belgium border in a town called Crecy. They took over a building next to City Hall. It had been the German's H.Q.

Matt found a good trunk that would hold their

jackets they were shipping home. A fellow M.P. sent Matt a note telling him not to return, there were angry Frenchmen looking for a short PFC and tall corporal that might have been M.P.s.

Matt was able to unload the rest of their script beyond the limit by buying black market fresh food. The food they traded with combat troops for war souvenirs.

The next few days were spent doing routine M.P. duty. When not directing traffic and streams of trucks of The Red Ball Express, they were patrolling the bars and busting heads of G.I.s letting off too much stress after drinking. Many they just locked up till somewhat sober and turned loose. There were times when they worked both day and night.

"Jeff, we got to get a break. Other M.P.s are taking off to look for those Kraut top brass. Catch a general or high ranking SS and it's a three-day pass to Paris. There's two green replacement M.P.s. What say I con them into taking over our tour this afternoon?"

"You spring it, and I'll find a jeep. I already have a rotor, points and fan belt."

Two hours of checking empty houses and barns had gained the boys nothing but the two chickens Jeff had liberated.

"I know a cook. I'll get him to cook them and keep one."

Then they saw him walking down the road, bold as can be. Never had the two seen such a distinguished uniform, gold shoulder pads, brass ribbons and buttons. He looked like a cross between a high-priced theater usher and a character from a Gilbert and Sullivan play. He had a fancy case on his side with its strap over one shoulder.

"That's a general for sure," cried Jeff.

When they cuffed him, he spoke only German and denied any understanding of English. His protests at their stopping him were mild.

At the headquarters building, they turned him in and were told to wait in the hall till the interpreter returned from lunch.

Soon a captain came out. "Congratulations, men," he said with a laugh," you captured a Prussian mailman. Now drive him back to where you found him."

Chastened, Jeff drove while Matt kept a close eye on the smiling mailman in the back seat.

Matt hit his palm on his forehead and then leaned over and whispered for Jeff to pull over near a barn. He pulled his .45 out and stuck it in the face of the mailman.

"What gives?" asked Jeff.

"I was watching his face in the rear mirror. He

understands English. I want to check out his bag. They might have missed something at H.Q. Cuff him."

The mailman shoved Jeff into Matt and reached into his bag. He was not as fast as Matt, who beat him to the draw, so to speak, as a cocked .45 was jammed in his nose while his hand had barely reached into his bag. He backed off and Jeff cuffed his hands behind his back.

They marched him into the barn, where Matt brushed the dust from a table and dumped the mailbag. The first thing to hit was a .9 mm Luger pistol. There were many envelopes that had stamps and handwritten addresses. Matt saw that some near the bottom were thick. He ripped one open over the cries of the mailman. Out came a stack of currency. They soon found more with money from several nations, including U.S. twenties and one hundred dollar denominations.

"Jackpot," said Jeff, as he started to pocket some of the dollars.

"Hold on, Buddy, we got to turn this in if we want a pass to Paris."

"All of it?"

"Okay, most." Matt then arranged the money and they settled for two hundreds and six twenties each. Plus, Matt had them each take a German Reichmark that had a one and many zeroes as a souvenir.

Now exposed, the German spoke, in excellent English. "I'm General Wolfgang Von Stumpf. Let me go and you can keep all the money, and I'll make you a map of where there are gems, gold and silver buried. The war is almost over. We will soon be fighting together against the Russians."

Matt turned his head and winked at Jeff. "Jeff, he's right. We fight and bleed for peanuts while the top brass are better paid, fed, and you can bet they're not going home empty handed. What'ya say?"

"First, I want to see a map or it's no deal."

Matt pocketed the Luger, undid the cuffs, and gave his pencil and pad to the general.

When he was done with the map, his hands were re-cuffed behind his back.

First, they both compared the map with what they recalled from maps they had seen. Matt said, "I'm satisfied. Turn around please."

The German turned around. Matt gave Jeff a signal they had used many times before. Jeff hit the German with a roundhouse right that knocked him down.

"Any more questions?" Matt asked the captain as the German general was led away. The contents of his mailbag were spread on a table. The captain asked his lieutenant to leave the room. Now there was just Jeff, Matt and the captain.

"Men, I'm very proud of you." He then said with a smile, "The G-2 that told us you had a mailman will be wiping egg off his face for days." He closed the door. "Just between us," he pointed to the stacks of money, "a lot of this will be pocketed by sticky fingers of several officers as it is processed. What the hell, here." And to their surprise, he gave two twenties to each of them.

"Now take your three-day passes to Paris and keep your mouths shut."

As they were almost out the door, he called them back. Jeff and Matt held their breath.

"Hey, you guys know anything about some guys passing off play money as the new script?"

Matt and Jeff shook their heads.

"I thought not. When the colonel heard about it, he said, 'Do I bust them or give them a medal?' Dismissed! Enjoy Paris."

THE PENCIL LIEUTENANT

At One Rockefeller Plaza, in an office of Smith Barney, on the wall of a vice president, there is the usual display of diplomas including an MBA from Yale, a B.S. in Communication from Northwestern, several certificates of training, and in a place of honor, a cherry-wood glass frame holding an Honorable Discharge from the U.S. Army. If you looked close, you could just see in a lower corner of that frame, a worn stub of a number two pencil.

Vietnam, the late '60s, the rain stopped, giving the men of the third platoon a brief spell of somewhat cooler weather before the sun turned the rain water into steam. A jeep slid and skidded in the mud, coming to a stop at the headquarters tent. Sergeant Carter opened the tent flap and saw the tall, clean second lieutenant adjust his tie as a private removed his duffle bag.

"No, shit, a Tie," said Carter to no one but the rank air. He returned the lieutenant's salute and stuck out his hand after checking that there was only a little mud on it.

"Welcome to the Third, Sir. I'm Sergeant Carter, platoon sergeant.

Before he could say a word, Lieutenant Second Class Lane spoke, with a force of absolute authority.

186

"Assemble the men, sergeant. I want to inspect my platoon."

"No can do, Sir. We just got back from six days in the brush. The men are scattered all over, some at chow, others at the dispensary, and most getting what sleep they can.

Before you could swat a bug, the sergeant grabbed the lieutenant by his arm and dragged him into the tent.

"Now listen, if you want to stay alive and get all of your body parts back home, I'm going to set you straight. See this pencil! That's what you are in charge of. This is my platoon! I'll give the orders to the men, you take that pencil and sign the papers we give you. CLEAR?!"

"You are an inch away from a charge of insubordination, sergeant!" said the startled lieutenant.

Sergeant Carter took a deep breath. He had been here many times before.

"Have a seat. Take a drink." He pushed a cold Coke from a cooler towards the officer. "I'll explain. You are lieutenant number four in the last six months. Take a minute and recall what the C.O. told you when you reported in."

When there was no answer, the sergeant continued. "It went like this. 'Welcome to Fire Base

G 59-8. You will take over third platoon. The first thing you should do is listen carefully to what Sergeant Carter says. Hell, Sir, I'm a full sergeant. And I listen to my PFCs that have been in the brush."

The new shave tail nodded in agreement, and decided to hear the sergeant out before setting him straight. No sorry looking mere sergeant was going to tell him how to fight a war.

Carter held up one finger.

"The first lieutenant that came here did not listen to me. He stood tall at the wrong time and went home in a body bag. The second one lasted a week till he didn't listen to one of the PFCs and stepped on a mine. He went home without half a leg, and I lost two good men getting him out. Number three listened. He lasted two months. He was just unlucky and got hit by incoming fire, right outside this bunker. That was last week. Did you notice how many replacements came on the flight with you? Why do you think only one was sent here to the third? I'll tell you. I don't lose as many men as the other platoons do. My newbies don't get sent out into the brush till they have had time to learn the ropes. When I take you for a walk around this hill, you will see that the Third has the strongest and best bunkers, firing positions and is the cleanest. That's what the new men do till I feel they are ready to go out. Now, don't say a word, let's take a walk."

Lieutenant Lane decided to put off taking charge. It would not hurt to let this sergeant show him around, and run things for a few more days. He would hold off implementing his ideas on how to fight the VC for a while.

Hill G 59-8 was a forward fire base. The top of a mile long ridge had been blasted off by the engineers, and bulldozed into a short landing strip. The jungle had been cleared for about five hundred meters on most sides. The steep west side was rocks and elephant grass all the way down to the Rao Duan River. Most attacks came from the east where the tree line was just out of rifle range. The combat engineers had dug in several 155 artillery pieces and made bunkers to hold ammunition, supplies, a make-shift hospital and a mess hall. Near the edge on all sides there were raised firing positions and eight deep bunkers, two for each platoon.

"What's that sad looking shed?" the lieutenant asked, as he pointed to a small metal and wood building with three steps, close to the east border.

"That's our common latrine. It's raised 'cause we ran out of places to bury the shit, so you crap into a half, a fifty-five gallon barrel. When it gets near full, we burn it off with gas or diesel oil. Have to do that on days when the wind comes from the east or west."

Back at the command bunker for the third platoon, the lieutenant unpacked his gear and studied the maps that Sergeant Carter gave him. Their base on top of this hill commanded one of the few east-west roads, and could use its big guns to support troops defending that road, and they could block VC movement on boats on the river below them to the west. Patrols would sweep the jungle around the base. The main problem was that the VC could get within easy mortar range any night they pleased. The base was always under the watchful eyes of the VC. This made it hard to set up ambush teams.

The lieutenant tried to be useful making reports and requisitioning supplies and learning the men. He saw that even Sergeant Carter really did listen to his PFCs and valued their advice, since they were out in the jungle more than he.

"Sergeant, I want to go on this next patrol. I have an idea, but need to get a first hand look at what's down there."

The sergeant agreed. It had been two weeks and the lieutenant had cooperated. It was a simple sweep. Ten men went out and broke into two groups, supporting each other and clearing mines and booby traps on the trails near the base. No shots were fired, but there were signs that the VC were moving around and it was found that they cleared overhanging tree limbs facing the base. It was plain they would deliver a mortar attack soon.

"Here's what I suggest. We go out with twelve men. As we cross the clearing bunched up, to make it hard to count them, we take extra body bags. Once we get into the jungle, we set up a strong position and draw their fire. Then we retreat carrying four body bags back loaded with brush and rocks. Four good men hide till dark and when we radio to them about where the mortars are, they lead our effort. We could have men ready to rush to their aid, and they would give us the element of surprise. What do you think?"

Sergeant Carter broke into a rare smile. "Damn, I got me a fighting lieutenant with a brain for a change. Just a few changes. We support the six not four men from the air with a gun ship, and during the fire fight, a few men must scream as if hit and call 'medic.' Please write up this plan and clear it with the C.O. Tell him I approve." This was the first time the lieutenant had ever heard Carter say please.

The C.O. set the next night for their ambush patrol. He sent two new men to third platoon.

Carter was on an inspection walk outside the fire base. One of the PFCs told the lieutenant that the "shit" barrel was full, as he pointed to the two green men that were standing around. Lieutenant Lane pointed to the wood latrine building and ordered the new men to burn off the stuff. But his orders were not clear. He said something about burning and the smell and high time. Next thing that happened was men yelling. The new men had set fire to not only the half barrels of crap, but to the whole toilet buildings. Foul smelly smoke was drifting all over the place. A token effort to save the building was made with a fire extinguisher. A slight breeze drifted the smoke towards the east.

The fire brought the C.O. who yelled, "Who the hell is responsible for this?"

Lieutenant Lane said, "Sorry, Sir, I sent two green newbies to burn the crap, and they got carried away. Or confused. It's my fault."

"Lieutenant, was your order spoken or written?"

"Sir? I didn't think that was the kind of detail that required a written order."

"I have a standing directive. It's in the instruction book they gave you. ALL OFFICERS WILL WRITE OUT IN FULL ALL ORDERS FOR THEIR FIRST 30 DAYS! I suggest you go back and read that material, and till I tell you otherwise, put everything in writing, then I will know who to blame and how to correct problems."

One of the PFCs spoke to Lieutenant Lane.

"Sir, one time the VC used smoke like that to get closer and shot the hell out of us with rockets."

"Think we should send out a fire team?"

"No! If I was you, I'd have the mortars zeros in

on the area where the smoke is close to the brush. A few rounds and they will get the idea and back off."

The sergeant in charge of the mortars only agreed after Lane put the request in writing. Lane wrote it out and made a mental note that if they killed any VC, he would cut a notch in his pencil.

Carter ran back from the west side when he heard the mortars fire. He chased some of his men to the firing pits and asked if the VC had hit the latrine and set it on fire. A very embarrassed Lane explained the burning latrine and was getting to the mortar fire when the C.O. stopped them and asked what the firing was about. When he saw Sergeant Carter, the C.O. ordered him to have his men dig a new ditch that would be used till the engineers could build a new toilet building.

"And dig that shit ditch in the third's area."

"Lieutenant, let's talk." Carter and Lane went into the bunker. "Don't take it too hard, burning the whole latrine. It's funny, but the PFC that talked you into firing the mortars was only half right. You should have waited till you could get some VC. The C.O. did not call off the body bag con patrol. He advised me that he would clear your going only if you gave me your word to stay close to me and do only what I say. He made it clear he's tired of writing letters home for lieutenants that get wasted."

Heavier than usual rains made them put off the

patrol.

"You see, Sir, with that much rain we lose more men to mines. They can't see them or walk where they should. I've seen good and careful men slide right onto a mine on a steep muddy trail. I'd like you to go to Saigon with Corporal Howard. He's my best scrounger. The only way you can get what you need is to go yourself or send a good man. You should have seen by now what supplies you have requested are not always what they send us. The corporal backed up with you and your pencil, I mean authority, should make a great team."

Corporal Howard was not what the lieutenant expected. He was a twenty year man, over forty, and wearing skull patches on his uniform.

"North Philly," was where he said he came from.

They left the supply depot for the city as soon as they got a jeep. The corporal drove. He stopped at a fruit stand and had the lieutenant watch the jeep. He came back from behind a curtain with two boxes of Cuban cigars.

"Now we can order our supplies and get when we need."

He passed out the cigars and joked with guards and supply depot staff. The lieutenant turned over his written request and watched as the clerk red lined out about a third of the items.

Corporal Howard, after looking around and seeing no officers, whispered to the private that took their order. "What you need to get rid of that I can take off your hands for double our order of claymore mines?" He pointed to a stack of wooden boxes.

"They still keep sending me BARs. They're just too heavy for most guys. They're packed four to a case. Take four off my hands and I'll find a way to double your supply of claymore mines."

"What other goodies you got, say if I took six boxes of BARs?"

"You take six and I'll throw in two cases of canned fruit cocktail, that's number six size, chow-hall cans."

He knew that these cans of fruit cocktail in sugar syrup were in demand for making of alcoholic drinks. What he did not know was that Corporal Howard saw the wood boxes as building material for making their bunkers stronger. The BARs could be used in the fixed firing positions where they would give greater firepower and range than the AR-15s. He would trade half of the BARs to other platoons.

The lieutenant and corporal returned in a helicopter overloaded with the BARs, their ammo, and a passenger. A photojournalist representing the *New York Times*, named Scott Miles, had been given permission to visit the firebase.

Miles was angry that he was not allowed to go with the lieutenant and Carter on their patrol.

The body bag con worked. Six men hid and the rest carried the fake body bags back. Their hide was saved by "Puff," the C-47 gun ship that used its vulcan-gatling to hold back the NVC. The next morning the six men caught the NVC as they were setting up their mortars. Their return to the fire base was not as successful as hoped, even with extra firepower from the BARs they had several wounded and Carter and the lieutenant led a squad to help them back.

They were just reaching the fire base when a NVC rocket exploded behind them. Carter was hit and knocked down, but unhurt thanks to his body armor. The lieutenant was not so lucky. A splinter of shrapnel went deep into the back of his knee.

"A million dollar wound," said one of the PFCs.

To make matters worse, the man from the *New York Times* had taken a picture of the crew carrying the body bags. He did not ask, he just assumed they held dead Marines. His story with the picture made the front page all over the nation, many times with the caption, Marine Patrol, half killed. There was no mention of the NVC that were killed.

Lieutenant Lane was loaded onto a chopper for evacuation.

As they shook hands, Carter said, "By the way, you never told me what the C.O. said about your detail burning the latrine. What did he say?"

Lieutenant Lane reached in his pocket and pulled his pencil. "He just said I should've used this."

SQUIRT'S ANGEL

"Hey you! Yes, you with the cutting torch. Crawl back outta dat hole. Seaman, that's an order." Navy SeaBee, Seaman First Class Fleming, called Squirt by his buddies, slowly backed out of the wrecked Jap barge and turned off the flame of his acetylene cutting torch. The closest thing to a uniform he wore was his faded and paper thin dungarees held up with a canvas cartridge belt that also held a 45 in a worn black holster. When he stood at his full five feet no inches, you could appreciate his nickname.

"Whadda ya want, Sir?"

The Lieutenant JG. (for Junior Grade), in his clean whites, took off his hat and wiped the sweat from his forehead.

"Did I see you get burned?" he asked using his most authoritative voice. As a young officer, at age twenty, he was uncomfortable giving orders to men well beyond his tender age.

"It wasn't anything, Sir. Happens all the time. I'm the only one that will fit in these tight places, so yeah, I get a few bits of hot metal dropped on me. The other welders don't mean it. I'll be fine."

He made a move to get back to work.

"Hold it, sailor, I didn't dismiss you. Don't they have asbestos protective shoulder pads you should be wearing?"

"No disrespect, Sir, but in this heat! Also, I'd never fit in the tight places. What I cut out, the welders are using to make the loading dock bigger. I have to keep at it or I'll be holding up the show."

"The show will have to wait. I'm sending you to the nurse over at the First Aid hut."

With a grin that would hold a dinner plate, his buddy, Seaman Ridge, used his cutting torch and pointed to the west.

"Yeah, can't not let the officer down. It's only a two-mile hike to the other side of the inlet. Give my love to Corpsman Tobin," said Seaman First Class Ridge.

This was on a small island in 1944; the SeaBees and a few Army engineers were all that were left of the invasion force. There was a handful of Marines sitting around in case any Japs should dig their way out of the caves that had been blasted shut. The island had no name, just a number, and was going to be made into a supply depot.

Seaman Ridge, as well as Squirt, had met Navy Corpsman Tobin who was there to meet their medical needs. His name was Virgil and he had breath so bad it would knock down a seagull at ten yards. Virgil Tobin had thick hairy arms covered with tattoos. No one would seek his care short of a bleeding wound or broken nose.

With dragging feet, Squirt went to his tent to get a blouse. While the daytime temperature regularly got over 110, you had to wear some semblance of a uniform unless actually at work. He walked a good pace once he made up his mind to get this Mickey-Mouse crap over with. To Squirt, most regulations that didn't pertain to is welding duties were Mickey-Mouse.

He had no trouble spotting a small building with a white painted door that had a red cross in the center. A sign read WALK-IN. He walked in as a spring slammed the door behind him. There was a cot and a washstand on one side. On the other, a cabinet with glass doors filled with bandages and medicine bottles. A white sheet hung from a wire across the back of the room. He saw no one. *"Great,"* he thought, *"I can go."* He was turning to leave when the sweetest voice he had ever heard spoke.

"Can I help you, sailor?" Coming out from behind the sheet was an angel, a real live female Navy nurse. Squirt had been at sea for fourteen months and the closest he had been to any woman was a well-worn Betty Grable pinup photograph. This was not only a live female nurse, she was a knockout, a blue-eyed blond with hair the color of ripe wheat. Her gleaming white uniform was strained by her greatly appreciated female attributes the nature of which sailors dreamed.

He couldn't speak. He stammered and after a pause, she raised her open palms in a gesture questioning what he wanted.

"They sent me here 'cause of a burn. It's nothing, just a bit from a welding spark. Where's Corpsman Tobin?"

"He was sent to escort some wounded. I'm here to replace him. I'm stationed on the hospital ship. I think he'll be back in a week or two, his gear is still here. Where is your burn?"

Squirt clumsily pointed over his shoulder to his back. He held his hat covering his crotch to hide where his blood pressure was building.

"I'll need your name, sailor. I'm Nurse Sally Thompson," she said as she pulled off his shirt.

"My name is...uh, Fleming, Robert, everybody calls me Squirt. It's okay with me, that's just a nickname."

"Where's your home, Seaman Fleming?"

"Cottonwood Creek, Kansas. It's close to Wichita."

Squirt started to ask her if she had ever been to Wichita, but his mouth was too dry. She had him sit on one of two folding chairs while she washed his back.

"You may think this is just a little burn, but in this climate, any break in the skin can get infected then ulcerate and become a major problem."

"Yes, nurse, I mean, Sir...Lieutenant. Are you telling me I should come back if I get burned again?"

"Consider that as an order. What are you doing? Are you getting enough to eat? You look too thin. And when was the last time you got a good night's sleep?" These questions she asked while taking a cloth cover off a bucket that was full of cold bottles of Coke. She took out two, gave him one, and sat on the cot with hers. She crossed her legs and supported herself with one hand. Using the Coke, she pointed to an open window.

"The Army Engineers promised me a fan, but I don't even have electricity if I did have a fan."

Squirt left walking a foot above the black sand of that island. He still had the Coke. As he put it to his lips to drink, he pressed hard and dreamed he was kissing her tiny red rosebud lips.

His buddies kidded him about going to the Corpsman with just a small burn.

"Putting in for a purple heart?"

That night he made a midnight requisition to the

huge warehouse where he found a fan in the office. He also took a roll of number ten wire. No one was in the First Aid hut when he slipped in through the window and left the fan. He was going to leave a note, but decided against it. The wire he placed under the hut till he could get a generator.

The next night he borrowed a jeep and found, on the other end of the island, a generator that had been used to light up the loading dock. To get it in the jeep he had to rig a rope pulley to slide it up a board covered with grease. Squirt got about an hour's sleep that night. He figured the Army engineers would know how to start the generator. He left it hooked up and supplied with three Jerry cans of gas. He wanted to tell her he had gotten the fan for her, but thought better. He would not get any chance to see her from the brig.

It took him several tries to get a respectable burn.

His buddies questioned his announcement that he had to go get his burn treated.

"Hey, there's no officer here now."

"Don't you guys know in this climate these things can ulcerate and cause real damage?" he said as he left for the nurse's hut. His buddies began to see a change in their small friend. At times he was a tiger at work, taking chances with no fear of the hot metal. He paid a guy to cut his hair and began to look after his uniform.

His next visit to the first aid hut, and one about every other day, made his buddies suspicious. And there were times he would not take part in the card games or bull sessions, but would sit and look at a sunset or the waves. He was well aware that enlisted men were forbidden to date or even talk to the female nurses except in the line of duty. But he could dream. He dreamed of taking his nurse, his angel, to his family farm. He would teach her to catch bluegill and catfish.

"Squirt gets burned and it's right off to the first aid hut. He's up to something. Maybe a still?"

"Nah! If the kid took a drink, we'd smelled it."

A few days later, Grant burned his elbow on a hot metal pipe. "I think I'll go see the first aid hut. Whadda ya think, Squirt, shall I go have this looked at?" He had been on Squirt's case, kidding and calling him a baby for his many trips to get first aid.

Squirt knew that Corpsman Tobin was back, but was not about to tell Grant. Not after all the kidding that was the price of the visits to his angel of a nurse.

"It's your elbow that's burned, you decide to go," Squirt replied.

Grant whispered to one of the other guys, "Maybe I'll find out what Squirt's been up to."

Seaman Grant opened the door and found Corpsman Tobin reading a copy of *Stars and Stripes*. "What's your problem?" he asked, his breath driving Grant back two feet.

"It's this burn. I don't want it to get infected or ulcerated." He showed the red spot on his elbow.

"You bothering me for that! Should call you guys sissy-bees not SeaBees. He laughed and enjoyed his pun, so he repeated it. "Come here, sissy-bee. Put some of this on it and get-out-a-here. Oh, by the way, sores get ulcerated in jungles, not on dry islands like this one." He handed a jar of ointment to Grant and returned to his paper.

Grant fumed from embarrassment all the way back across the island. For a few days he gave Squirt all the dirtiest jobs. He also noted that even when hit by a hot spark, Squirt did not go to the First Aid hut any more.

When the welding crew finished with the loading dock, they were moved across the island where some buildings were being made. The Army engineers had pulled out. One of the first to be built was a bathhouse and latrine for the female staff from the hospital ship that was docked there.

A mountain of 16 gauge galvanized sheet metal was being transformed into open sided buildings for the wounded. The men mounted a water tank on top of the female latrine to make a shower. They stood sheets of two by eight galvanized sheet metal in a wrap-around square with a walk-in door that prevented anyone from looking in. Buckets with many nail holes and fire hose for pipes completed the shower. When it was done, a high wind began to work loose some of the metal roofing sheets. The nurses said the noise bothered the wounded. Because of his light weight, Squirt was sent to do a better job nailing down the roof. That involved using a sharp punch and strong blows with a hammer to make holes in the metal roofing so long nails could be driven into the wood frame. By the time the metal roof was cool enough for Squirt to work on, it was almost dark. He saw that it would take many more nails to get the roof to stay flat in the wind. He was reaching for a nail when he heard water run. Below him a nurse was starting to take a shower. There was only one small light bulb mounted to the side away from the splashing water. Like a true-blue sailor, he said not a word. From his viewpoint on the roof, he could see down to her waist; she had her back to him. He moved to a part of the roof out of her sight where he could just peek over the edge without being seen. He started to drive one more nail when she turned, facing his direction. The hammer hit his thumb right on the knuckle. Squirt rolled farther away from the edge and, in a soft voice, said a few words that he did not learn in Sunday School. He gave it a lot of thought, deciding to take another peek. If it was his nurse, he would slide back and wait till she was gone. It was a red haired nurse who was joined by a very short one with tiny breasts. He waited till they were all gone and then, working in the dark, tried to put in the last nails. He hit the same place on his thumb while trying to make a new hole in the roof sheeting. With that he quit.

The next morning his thumb swelled and he was sent to the hospital ship to have it x-rayed. It was broken and would take weeks to heal.

At morning roll call the men always lined up with the tallest on the far right. Squirt on the left end was closest to the loading dock. As they waited for their commander, Squirt saw that the cutter from the hospital ship docked, but no one got out. It just sat there. The commander was accompanied by a Lieutenant, who was a medical officer, and Corpsman Tobin.

"Men, there is an acute shortage of whole blood for the wounded from last week's battle at Tarawa. Under the direction of Corpsman Tobin, those that can will be asked to give blood. Take over, Tobin."

"Except for any that have or had malaria within the last month, and a few that I will not name that are being treated for a...social disease, you are asked to donate blood. All that give will get a twenty-four hour duty excuse. The first twenty of you volunteers get on that cutter and go to the hospital ship. The rest line up at the First Aid hut after the Captain dismisses ya."

Squirt was the first to get into the boat, but that made him the last one out. By the time he was done giving blood, they had run out of sailors and SeaBees and were doing the hospital staff.

Squirt was escorted to a small mess room that was being used as a waiting lounge. He was told to have a drink, take a seat and would be returned for in an hour. He picked at a bit of cotton and tape on his arm—it itched. He was the only one in the room when who should come in with her own bit of cotton and tape but Nurse Lieutenant Sally Thompson. His angel gave him a smile and a weak wave. Her face was almost as pale as her white uniform. His eyes were on her when he saw her knees start to bend as she reached to put back a juice cup. She was about to faint! Squirt leaped across the room and caught her in his arms as she was halfway to the floor. Then it happened. The effort was too much for him. He too fainted. In falling, he grabbed at the table bringing it down on top of them.

Squirt was having the best dream of his life—he was holding his angel. It was so real, then a wet cloth wiped his face. He opened his eyes to see four of the medical staff around him. They were laughing. He tried to rise and found he was on a table.

"You both fainted," a voice said. He heard a female voice speak his name. A nurse moved aside and Nurse Thompson on the next table waved at him. Her face was still white as she was rolled away.

"Take him to ward B and keep him in bed till his blood pressure is back to normal."

"Sir, please sign this. It's his twenty-four hour duty excuse."

"Change it to forty-eight hours. Hell, he saved one of my staff from hitting the floor."

For most nights and some days, Squirt's dreams started with what it was like to hold his angel. He took a lot of kidding about the fainting. Grant went so far as to make him a paper purple heart for the bump on the back of his head. He didn't mind. He figured he was the only enlisted man on the island to have touched a live female, and he had held one.

The men were all excited. An Ensign who was in charge of morale came up with a co-ed softball game. There would be four nurses on each team. A drawing was held to pick the men players, except for two ex-pro ballplayers who were assigned one to each team. Squirt traded his monthly cigarette rations for extra chances in the drawing. He made the team. When no one wanted to be catcher, he was volunteered. The coach promised he would not have to catch the whole game if his sore thumb hurt. But he could not take another position as there were too many men that wanted to play. He was just able to squeeze the bandaged digit into his glove.

He was guarding home plate when there was a

ball hit to right field. Nurse Sally Thompson tried to run home from third base. Squirt caught the ball while she was a good six feet away from him. He heard her coach yell at her to run him down. "Make him drop the ball!" She put her head down and charged. Squirt kept the ball in his glove and tagged her with it on her hip, but he instinctively put up his right hand. As she fell into and on top of him, that hand made firm contact with her left breast. In fact, it was still there engulfing it as she began to roll off of him. His teammates yelled, "At-a-boy, Squirt." Instead of the slap he expected, she playfully kissed his cheek and jumped up. Squirt stood and to his teammates yelled, "I'm catching the rest of the game!"

THE END

Official Army Recipe for

Chipped Beef on Toast

#55 Beef, dried, chipped, or sliced, on toast.

From the 1943 Army Manual 10-405, page 339.
Feeds 120 people.

7 Pounds chipped or sliced dried beef
2 bunches parsley, chopped fine
2 pounds fat, butter preferred
1/2 ounce pepper
1 pound flour, browned in fat
4 gallons beef stock
4 cans milk, evaporated
120 slices bread, about 12 pounds

Melt fat in pan, add flour. Cook a few minutes to brown the flour. Add milk and beef stock, stirring constantly to prevent lumping. Add dried beef and cook five minutes. Add parsley and pepper. Serve hot on toast.